Barbara Cartland, ... n, playwright, lectu ... sonality, has now ... s had a number of l ... graphical ones, inc ... Ronald Cartland, w ... ...liament to be killed in the wa... ...ook has a preface by Sir Winston Churchill.

In private life, Barbara Cartland is a Dame of Grace of St. John of Jerusalem, and one of the first women, after a thousand years, to be admitted to the Chapter General. Chairman of the St. John Council for Hertfordshire, she has served in the St. John Ambulance Brigade for thirty-five years.

Barbara Cartland has fought for better conditions and salaries for midwives and nurses, and, as President of the Hertfordshire Branch of the Royal College of Midwives, she has been invested with the first Badge of Office ever given in Great Britain, which was subscribed to by the midwives themselves. She has also championed the cause of old people and founded the first Romany Gypsy Camp in the world. It was christened 'Barbaraville' by the gypsies.

Barbara Cartland is deeply interested in Vitamin Therapy and is President of the National Association for Health.

BARBARA CARTLAND

THE CURSE OF THE CLAN

Pan Original
Pan Books London and Sydney

Author's Note. The State Visit of King George IV to Edinburgh in 1822 organised by Sir Walter Scott was an unqualified success.

There is a portrait of the King, by Sir David Wilkie, in full Highland dress, wearing the Royal Stewart tartan in which he appeared at the levee at Holyrood Palace.

Although His Majesty, who always liked to dress up, was delighted with his appearance those who saw him found the effect of the flesh-coloured tights which he wore under his kilt somewhat ludicrous.

My descriptions of the festivities in the Scottish Capital are factual and come from a book published in Edinburgh the same year.

First published 1977 by Pan Books Ltd,
Cavaye Place, London SW10 9PG
© Cartland Promotions 1977
ISBN 0 330 25261 5
Printed and bound in Great Britain by
Hazell Watson & Viney Ltd, Aylesbury, Bucks

Chapter One
1822

"It's very pleasant to see you here again, Mr. Falkirk."

"It has been a long time, Mrs. Barrowfield – let me think now – it must be at least six years."

"Seven to be exact since you last paid us a visit. But, as I always says, I never forget a face or a friend, and I've always looked on you as a friend, Mr. Falkirk."

"I am honoured, Mrs. Barrowfield."

The Scotsman gave the large, blowsy woman a slight bow, then clearing his throat as if he intended to get down to business, he said:

"You must wonder why I have called on you today."

"It did cross my mind," Mrs. Barrowfield replied with a laugh. "After all I could hardly flatter myself it was to see me bright eyes. Nevertheless, we must celebrate."

She rose as she spoke from the ancient creaking chair at the side of the hearth and crossed the room to open a cupboard.

From it she brought out a bottle of port and two glasses and setting them on a round tray brought them towards her visitor. She placed them beside him on a table which he looked at anxiously as it seemed decidedly unsteady.

The room in which they were sitting was poorly and sparsely furnished and badly in need of a coat of paint.

However, it was littered with cheap knick-knacks such as middle-aged women collect and the brightly burning fire gave it some semblance of cosiness.

"Will you play host, Mr. Falkirk?" Mrs. Barrowfield asked with just a touch of coquetry in her words.

He picked up the bottle of port, glanced at the label apprehensively and poured Mrs. Barrowfield a full glass and himself a little over a quarter.

"You're very abstemious," his hostess remarked.

"In my position it is essential to keep a clear head," Mr. Falkirk replied.

"That I can understand," Mrs. Barrowfield conceded, "and how is His Grace?"

There was a little pause before Mr. Falkirk replied:

"It is on His Grace's instigation that I am here."

"His Grace's?" Mrs. Barrowfield raised her eyebrows. "I was hoping you'd come on an errand of mercy from the Duchess."

Mr. Falkirk looked surprised and Mrs. Barrowfield explained:

"His Grace's mother, Duchess Anne, took a great interest in the Orphanage, as I'm sure you remember. We received turkeys at Christmas and seldom a year passed that she did not entrust me with extra money to be spent on improvements. But with her death all that came to an end."

"I must admit her contributions to the Orphanage had escaped my notice," Mr. Falkirk remarked.

"I thought perhaps they had," Mrs. Barrowfield replied with a note of reproach in her voice, "but I'd hoped that the new Duchess would carry on the tradition."

Mrs. Barrowfield took another sip of port before she said:

"After all, it's very much in the family, isn't it? The Orphanage was started when Duchess Harriet, His Grace's grandmother, found that one of her kitchen-maids was 'in the family way', and rather than turn her out into the snow, built 'The Orphanage of the Nameless'."

She laughed.

"Those were the days, Mr. Falkirk, before the war when there was plenty of money and generous hands to dispense it."

Mr. Falkirk shook his head.

"Things are not so easy now, Mrs. Barrowfield, as I am sure you are aware."

"You don't have to tell me that," Mrs. Barrowfield said sharply. "I pinch and save, save and pinch, it's nothing but endless cheese-paring. The income that the Orphanage receives is just the same, but prices have gone up. Food is double what it was when I was a girl."

"I am sure that is true," the Scotsman murmured.

"When I came here to help the Matron I was fifteen and already had three years experience in another Home. I thought I was bettering myself."

Mrs. Barrowfield laughed raucously.

"I assure you, Mr. Falkirk, I had no intention of spending the rest of my days in this place, but this is where I be ended up and now I am Matron and with little or no help because we can't afford it."

"I had no idea that things were so difficult, Mrs. Barrowfield," Mr. Falkirk said. "Why have not the Guardians of the Orphanage written to His Grace?"

"Them!" Mrs. Barrowfield exclaimed rudely. "They're either dead or don't care!"

She saw the surprise on Mr. Falkirk's face and explained:

"Colonel McNab died three years ago, Mr. Cameron has been in ill health and is nigh on eighty, Lord Hirchington lives in the country and I haven't seen a sight or sign of him since Her Grace died."

"I can only promise," Mr. Falkirk answered, "that I will bring your position to the notice of His Grace as soon as I return to Scotland."

"I'd be very grateful if you would," Mrs. Barrowfield said in a different tone. "Do you know how many children I've got here at the moment?"

Mr. Falkirk shook his head.

"Thirty-nine!" Mrs. Barrowfield cried. "Thirty-nine, and practically no-one to look after them except myself. It's not right, that it's not! I'm getting on in years. Things aren't as easy for me as they used to be."

She drank down her glass of port and reached for the bottle.

Looking at the high colour of her face, the puffiness under her eyes, and the two or three extra chins which had developed since he last saw her, Mr. Falkirk guessed that Mrs. Barrowfield consoled herself constantly.

And if it was not the cheap port with which he had no

intention of ruining his stomach, he thought it would be gin which was quite rightly, in his opinion, known as 'mother's ruin.'

But nothing of what he was thinking showed itself in his calm expression as he sat in an arm-chair facing the Matron of the Orphanage and thinking that it was time he came to the point of his visit.

He was a tall, well-built man and had in his youth been outstandingly handsome.

With his hair greying at the temples and with a spare figure without an ounce of extra flesh he looked extremely distinguished and as the Duke of Arkcraig's Comptroller was much admired.

"I will certainly put your problems in front of His Grace," he repeated, "but what I came to ask you. . ."

He was interrupted before he could go further by Mrs. Barrowfield saying:

"You can tell His Grace that we're losing our reputation for supplying strong, healthy apprentices for those who need them. Only last week the owner of several tailoring shops came to see me and said:

" 'I want two of your best lads, Mrs. Barrowfield, and none of that knock-kneed anaemic rubbish you gave me last year.'

'What happened to the boys I let you have?' I asked.

'God knows!' he replied. 'Always ailing and snivelling, they were no use to me. I turned them off – and without a reference!' "

Mr. Falkirk looked grave.

"That is certainly something that should not happen, Mrs. Barrowfield, from an Orphanage which has been under the direct patronage of His Grace's family for over thirty years."

"That's exactly what I'm saying to you, Mr. Falkirk," Mrs. Barrowfield said. "It's an aspersion, as you might say, on His Grace's reputation, and even though you lives far away from us we have a great respect for Scotland and its noblemen."

"Thank you, Mrs. Barrowfield."

"That's why I was hoping," Mrs. Barrowfield continued, "that you could persuade the new Duchess to visit us."

"The Duchess is dead!"

"Dead?"

Mrs. Barrowfield's mouth opened and she looked, Mr. Falkirk thought, not unlike a surprised turkey-cock.

"Yes, dead," he said quietly. "Her Grace died a few weeks ago in France."

"Well, I never! You could knock me down with a feather! And her little more than a bride. Let me see now – she and His Grace couldn't have been married for more than a year."

"Ten months to be exact," Mr. Falkirk said in a dry voice.

"And now, poor lady, she has gone to her Maker! It seems a crying shame – it does really! And I never so much as sets eyes on her."

There was silence. Then as if he feared that Mrs. Barrowfield was about to ask a number of questions Mr. Falkirk said:

"His Grace has gone North and he asked me when I followed him to bring with me one of your orphans."

"One of my orphans?" Mrs. Barrowfield ejaculated. "I suppose His Grace wants one of the lads to work in the kitchen or in the pantry. Let me think ..."

"No, that was not His Grace's instruction," Mr. Falkirk interrupted. "He requires one of your girls, but she must be over sixteen."

"Over sixteen? You must be joking!" Mrs. Barrowfield exclaimed. "You know as well as I do, Mr. Falkirk, we don't keep them a day over twelve, if we can help it. Push them out younger, if we can."

She paused before she went on:

"And although I says it as shouldn't, the girls from here are noted as having good manners. At least they know how to speak with respect for their elders and betters, which is more than you can say for most young people to-day."

"That is true enough," Mr. Falkirk agreed, "but His Grace was quite certain you would be able to supply him with the type of young girl he needs."

"I always understood from the Duchess Harriett that you had all the young people in Scotland you needed," Mrs. Barrowfield said. "Her Grace took two of my girls once when the house in London was open. Very pleased I believe she was with them."

She smiled with an excess of self-gratification and went on :

"One of them came back to see me years later. She'd married a footman. Pretty bit, she was. I always thought she'd get herself married if she could find a man who'd overlook the unfortunate circumstances of her birth."

"You are quite certain you have no-one of the right age?" Mr. Falkirk insisted.

"Quite certain!" Mrs. Barrowfield answered. "The children here now are mostly very young and Heaven knows it's difficult enough looking after them and keeping them clean. What I'd do without Tara I don't know!"

"Tara?" Mr. Falkirk asked. "Is that the girl who let me in?"

"Yes, that'll be her. She looks after the little ones. Spoils them, I always say, but you can't put an old head on young shoulders."

Mrs. Barrowfield gave another of her loud laughs.

"It was very different with the old Matron. She believed in birching the children to keep them quiet. Good, bad or indifferent, she beat them all and I must say I often think her methods were better than mine. I'm too kind – that's the trouble with me."

"I am sure the fact that you are merciful to these unfortunate children is in your favour, Mrs. Barrowfield," Mr. Falkirk said, "but we were talking about Tara."

"I was just saying . . ." Mrs. Barrowfield began, then she stopped. "You're not suggesting . . . you're not intending . . ."

She put her empty glass down on the table with a bang.

"No, Mr. Falkirk, I'll not stand for it, that I won't! You

are not taking Tara from me. She's the only person in this place I can rely on. Who else do I have coming in? A couple of decrepit old women who can't get work elsewhere and are more trouble than they're worth, and I'm hard put to pay them as it is. You can take any of the children you like, the whole lot if it suits you, but not Tara!"

"How old is she?" Mr. Falkirk asked.

"Now let me see ... she must be nigh on eighteen. Yes, that'll be right. It was 1804 when she came here, a year after hostilities started up again with that devil Napoleon. I remember it because a terrible winter it was, and food went up with a jump. Coal was double the price!"

"So Tara is nearly eighteen," Mr. Falkirk said. "I am afraid, Mrs. Barrowfield, that if there is no-one else I must follow His Grace's instructions and take her with me to Scotland."

"Over my dead body!" Mrs. Barrowfield said violently. "I'll not have it, Mr. Falkirk. I'll not be left with thirty-nine screaming, unruly children, many of whom cannot even look after themselves."

She drew in her breath and became so crimson in the face that the Scotsman watching her was afraid she might have a stroke.

"If Tara goes – I go. You can put that in your pipe and smoke it!"

As if her legs would no longer hold her she sat down in the arm-chair to fan herself with a piece of paper she picked up from the table.

"I am sorry, Mrs. Barrowfield, to upset you," Mr. Falkirk said, "but you know as well as I do that I have to obey His Grace's instructions."

"It's not fair!" Mrs. Barrowfield replied in a voice which was suspiciously near to tears. "It's not fair! I'm messed about and put upon and nobody cares what happens to me! His Grace has enough girls in Scotland without taking the only one that's any use from the Orphanage dedicated to the memory of his dead grandmother."

Mrs. Barrowfield's voice broke and hastily Mr. Falkirk poured out another glass of port and put it into her hand.

She took it from him gratefully and having drunk half of it at a gulp lay back in her chair gasping for breath and fighting for self-control.

"I promise you one thing," Mr. Falkirk said quietly, "I will leave you enough money to employ some better help than you have at the moment and I will make it my duty, as soon as I return to Scotland to see that a larger grant is made by His Grace for the upkeep of this Orphanage."

He felt that his words placated Mrs. Barrowfield to a certain extent, but she continued to stare into the fire breathing heavily.

"Perhaps you could tell me what you know about this girl," Mr. Falkirk asked. "Has she another name?"

"Another name?" Mrs. Barrowfield repeated scornfully. "Have you forgotten, Mr. Falkirk? This is The Orphanage of the Nameless. Of course she has no other name, nor have any of the rest of the wretched creatures who are pushed in on me day after day, week after week."

She snorted before she went on :

" 'I've got another little bastard for you,' Dr. Harland says to me only last week. 'Well you can keep it,' I answers. 'I've not another hole or corner to put a mouse in, let alone a child.'

'Come along, Mrs. Barrowfield,' he says. 'You're a kind woman and you wouldn't want to see this scrap of humanity end up in the river.'

'I don't care where it ends up,' I replied, 'it's not coming here, and nothing you can say, Doctor, will make me change my mind.' "

"Did he take it away?" Mr. Falkirk asked.

"No, it joined the rest," Mrs. Barrowfield answered in a weary voice. "I thought I'd convinced him there was no room, but Tara tells him that the baby could share a cot with another and so she squeezes them in together.

"I said to her afterwards: 'You're a fool! You're only giving yourself more work.' "

"But she did not mind?"

"It's me who has to mind!" Mrs. Barrowfield said sharply. "It's me that has another mouth to feed and not a penny piece to pay for the food they gobbles up. 'Gold-dust — that's what you're eating,' I've said to the older ones over and over again, but they're always whining and saying they're hungry."

Mr. Falkirk was drawing a wallet from the inner pocket of his well-cut travelling coat.

He took out some notes and laid them on the table in front of Mrs. Barrowfield.

"Here is twenty pounds," he said, "and it only has to last you until I have been able to reach Scotland and make better arrangements for the future."

He saw the glint of greed in the woman's eyes and wondered how much of the money would be spent on food for the orphans and how much on drink. But for the moment, he told himself there was nothing he could do but placate this blowsy, drink-sodden woman.

"Before you send for Tara, will you tell me what you know of her?" he asked.

"You really intend to take her away?"

"I am sorry, Mrs. Barrowfield, there is nothing else I can do unless you have another girl of suitable age."

Mrs. Barrowfield made a gesture of helplessness and said in a sulky tone:

"What do you want to know?"

"The actual day she came here. You keep records, I suppose?"

He saw the woman's eyes flicker and knew that if she had records they had certainly not been kept up to date for some time and doubtless he would learn very little from them.

Hastily, and he was sure it was because she wished to divert his attention Mrs. Barrowfield said:

"As it happens, Tara is different from the other children. She was born here. Born in this very building."

"How did that happen?"

"You may well ask. It was in the summer of 1804, just a little later in the year than now, the beginning of July, I think. I was sitting where I am at this moment when I hears a rat-tat enough to wake the dead, on the outside door. I jumps to my feet – I was younger in those days and could move quicker – and goes to see what the noise is all about."

Mrs. Barrowfield paused to finish her port, before she continued:

"There was quite a crowd outside and two men supporting a woman who was either dead or unconscious."

"What had happened?" Mr. Falkirk asked.

"There'd been an accident – a carriage had knocked her down in the street. The wheel had passed over her, but the coachman had driven on without stopping."

Mrs. Barrowfield held out her glass invitingly and Mr. Falkirk refilled it.

"That's them private coachmen all over – arrogant and overbearing, they be, and they don't care who suffers."

"Do go on with the story," Mr. Falkirk begged.

"Well, they carried the woman in and I sends a boy for the Doctor. He only lived three streets away. That was a Doctor Webber who was attending the Orphanage in those days. Disagreeable man – I never cared for him!"

"And the woman?" Mr. Falkirk asked trying to keep Mrs. Barrowfield to the point.

"I thought she was dead," Mrs. Barrowfield said, "but then before the Doctor arrives she begins groaning and moaning and finally I realise to my astonishment that she's in labour."

"You did not notice at first that she was pregnant?"

"As a matter of fact, I didn't," Mrs. Barrowfield confessed. "Perhaps I wasn't as observant then as I am now. She was wearing a loose gown and being a slight creature she didn't show it as a heavier woman might have done."

"What happened?" Mr. Falkirk asked.

"It was hours before the Doctor got here. They couldn't find him, or he wouldn't come. Heaven only knows what the explanation was. But I did my best and the baby was almost in the world before he even walks through the door."

Mrs. Barrowfield spoke scathingly. Then she said:

"Casual and off-hand he was about the whole thing. You know what Doctors are like when there's not a fat fee about. Anyway he delivers the baby and a nice mess he makes."

Mrs. Barrowfield sipped her port ruminatively, as if she were looking back at the past.

"I'd never been present at a confinement before. It both shocked and embarrassed me. I've never had children of my own, you see, not ever having been married."

Mr. Falkirk made no comment.

He remembered that it was a question of courtesy to give the Matron of an Orphanage the prefix of 'Mistress', whether or not she was entitled to it.

"Anyway," Mrs. Barrowfield went on, "the Doctor puts the baby down and says: 'That'll live if you take care of it, but the mother's dead!'"

"He could not save her?"

"If you ask me he didn't try," Mrs. Barrowfield sniffed, "and it's only when I looks at the mother before they comes to take her away for burial that I realises how young she is and in fact different from what I might have expected."

"What do you mean by different?" Mr. Falkirk asked.

"Well, if I didn't suppose to the contrary since no-one seemed to be worried about her or care whether she was alive or dead, I'd have said she was a lady. She certainly looked as if she was of gentle birth. Pretty, she was, with red hair and a white skin and clothes that must have cost a pretty penny, there's no doubt about that."

"Did you keep any of them?"

Mrs. Barrowfield shook her head.

"Nothing gets kept in this place. The orphans will steal anything they can get hold of in the winter when it's cold, and I expect her petticoats if she had any – they weren't fashionable at that time – were torn up as bandages. There's always one of those little varmints bleeding in some part of his anatomy."

"And there was nothing to distinguish her or give you an indication who she might have been?"

"As far as I knows the Doctor made enquiries," Mrs. Barrowfield said. "Looking for his fee, he was, if you asks me. He told me he'd asked if there had been any notification of a missing person in the neighbourhood, but nobody comes here to look for the baby, so I surmises he had no reply."

"Why did you name her Tara?" Mr. Falkirk asked.

"That was just what I was about to tell you," Mrs. field replied. "You asked if the dead·woman had any identification on her? She'd not so much as a handbag although if she had it would have been stolen when she was knocked down in the street."

Mrs. Barrowfield paused for effect and then went on:

"I can tell you one thing she didn't have and that was a wedding-ring! It may have been intentional that she'd come to the right place with her nameless child."

"Why did you name it Tara?"

"That was just what I was about to tell you," Mrs. Barrowfield answered. "The dead woman had a locket round her neck! I suppose you'll think I'm sentimental but I kept it even though if I'd had a bit of common sense I'd have sold it. Even a shilling or two would have helped at times when food was short."

"May I see the locket?" Mr. Falkirk asked.

If he found himself irritated by Mrs. Barrowfield's garrulous manner and the way she wandered from the point, he showed no sign of it.

His face was expressionless as she rose unsteadily to her feet to·go once again to the·piece of furniture from which she had taken the bottle of port.

It was a badly made, cheap cupboard supported on a table which contained two drawers.

Mrs. Barrowfield pulled open one of them and from where he was sitting Mr. Falkirk could see it was filled with bills, some creased ribbon, hair-combs, patterns of material, and a number of nameless objects which could be of little significance and no value.

Mrs. Barrowfield foraged about in the back of the drawer and finally came back with a small trinket-box in her hand.

"This is where I keeps my treasures," she said with an

ugly laugh. "As you can imagine, I've not many of them, and if I left them lying about those young devils would soon have their fingers on them."

She sat down again on the chair and opened the box on her ample lap.

Mr. Falkirk could see that it contained a number of loose blue beads from what had once been a necklace.

There was also a brooch without a pin, cheap bangles of the type which could be bought for a few pence in any fair-ground, and a piece of withered mistletoe which he thought must be a souvenir of Mrs. Barrowfield's youth, although it was hard at the moment to imagine her experiencing any form of romance.

"Why here it is!" she exclaimed.

She rummaged under the beads and brought out a small locket attached to a chain.

"That was round the poor woman's neck," she said holding it out to Mr. Falkirk.

It was gold, not of good quality and could not have cost very much money.

Inscribed on the outside was the word 'Tara' and when he opened the locket it contained a curl of dark brown hair.

"Honest – that's what I am!" Mrs. Barrowfield said. "As I told you, Mr. Falkirk, any other woman would have sold it, but I always thought perhaps one day it'd come in useful, and sure enough you're finding it interesting."

"I am indeed, Mrs. Barrowfield," Mr. Falkirk said, "and you will understand that I would like to take it with me."

"I can hardly imagine His Grace would be interested in such a trumpery," Mrs. Barrowfield said. "Why does he want the girl taken to Scotland? You haven't told me that yet."

"To tell you the truth I do not know, Mrs. Barrowfield," Mr. Falkirk replied. "I am merely obeying the orders His Grace gave before he left for the North."

"It seems strange to me," Mrs. Barrowfield said.

Mr. Falkirk agreed with her, but he was not prepared to admit it.

"Now perhaps," he said in his quiet voice, "you would send for Tara. I should like to make her acquaintance."

"When will you be taking her with you?" Mrs. Barrowfield asked.

There was a sharp note in her voice, but having put down the trinket-box she picked up the notes from the table and Mr. Falkirk was quite certain they were tangible consolation.

"I am leaving this afternoon," he replied. "As I pass the door after leaving Arkcraig House I can pick up Tara."

"She's travelling with you in your carriage?"

"There is no other way for her to journey North, and as I do not anticipate she will have much luggage we should not be overcrowded."

"Luggage! She'll have little enough of that!" Mrs. Barrowfield replied.

"If I could just see her before I leave ... ?" Mr. Falkirk said rising to his feet.

Mrs. Barrowfield however remained sitting in her chair.

"I feels a bit faint after hearing the bad news you've brought me," she said. "Just go to the door and shout her name. She'll hear you right enough."

Mr. Falkirk realised that Mrs. Barrowfield's faintness was due to over-indulgence.

He therefore made no protest but walked across the room and opening the door let himself out into the dim, ugly hall.

To furnish it there was only the deal table on which he had left his hat, and a hard chair on which he had laid his cloak when he first arrived.

On either side of the hall he could hear the sound of noisy voices and from above up the uncarpeted stairs the wailing of small children.

He had an instinctive feeling that he would find Tara with the children who were crying. He climbed the stairs slowly, holding onto the banister that not only wanted polishing but also mending, and finally reached the landing.

The Orphanage was built in two stories and when it was

completed on the Duchess Harriet's instructions it had been greatly admired as a model of its kind.

But Mr. Falkirk realised that thirty years had not only made the building out of date, it had also made the onslaught of time very obvious on the interior.

Perhaps it was only in the last few years, he thought, that the worst damage had occurred.

There were broken window-panes boarded up instead of being replaced with glass, there were floor-boards which were a danger to step on. There were doors that were swinging on their hinges because they lacked any form of fastening.

He took in these things at a glance and opening the door from where the noise came found himself in a long dormitory which smelt of dirt, unwashed children and a number of other things to which he had no wish to put a name.

There was a row of beds each side of the long room and the children were either lying crying forlornly in them or tumbling about with each other, screaming as they did so, and seeming to Mr. Falkirk to be very inadequately clothed.

At the far end of the room, nursing a very small baby in her arms, was the girl he had noticed when she let him into the house.

She was wearing a grey cotton gown with a white collar and a tight-fitting grey cap which he had recognised as the uniform chosen by the Duchess Harriet for her orphans.

It was certainly plain and proclaimed that the wearer was quite obviously an object of charity.

As Mr. Falkirk proceeded down the dormitory he realised that the children tumbling about on the beds all had their heads cropped close, and remembered that again was a requirement of those who had the privilege of being cared for in The Orphanage of the Nameless.

When he reached Tara she rose from the wooden stool on which she had been sitting, still holding the baby in her arms, and curtsied to him politely.

Mr. Falkirk looked at her searchingly for the first time. She was very thin, he thought, so thin he was quite certain it was the result of inadequate feeding, and the bones of her chin sharpened as she turned her face towards him.

Her eyes were very large and were a dark blue, fringed by thick eye-lashes which seemed to be gold at the roots but darkened almost dramatically at the ends as they curled upwards.

Such eyes might have been attractive, Mr. Falkirk thought, in a girl who was not so painfully thin that her cheek-bones stood out with hollows beneath them which made her seem almost like an unfledged bird.

"I wish to talk to you, Tara," he said.

She looked up at him in surprise. Then with what he thought was an unexpectedly soft and musical voice she said to the other children:

"Be quiet, dears, we have a visitor and he wishes to speak to me. If you sit on your beds and do not make a sound, I will tell you a story as soon as he has gone."

This was obviously a treat that they all desired for almost immediately the noise stopped. The children, who Mr. Falkirk guessed must be between the ages of four and seven, sorted themselves out on various beds and mattresses and sat there watching him wide-eyed, doubtless impatient for his departure.

The baby Tara held in her arms began to cry. She rocked it and slipped its thumb into its mouth so that it too was silent.

She looked up at Mr. Falkirk.

"Yes, Sir? You wanted to speak to me, Sir?"

"I am taking you away, Tara."

He saw her eyes widen and there was sudden fear in them.

"Oh, no, Sir! I cannot leave the children! Have you told Mrs. Barrowfield?"

"I have told her."

"And she agrees?" Tara asked incredulously.

"She has no alternative but to let you go. The Duke of Arkcraig has ordered that you should come with me to Scotland."

"To ... Scotland?"

There was no doubt now of the astonishment in Tara's voice and she added:

"I ... I thought you meant I was to be ... apprenticed."

"I do not know what you are to do," Mr. Falkirk said honestly. "All I know is that the Duke has asked for you, and it is by his orders that I must take you with me this afternoon when I leave London."

She looked round the dormitory helplessly as if she half-thought she could bring the children with her.

"I have given Mrs. Barrowfield enough money to engage someone to replace you," Mr. Falkirk said.

Then he too looked at the quiet children watching him and realised that it would be difficult, if not impossible, to replace what Tara meant in their lives.

It was obvious that Mrs. Barrowfield contributed little or nothing towards their comfort and well-being.

He was a bachelor and he had had little to do with children, but he would have been a very unimaginative man if he had not guessed that the only affection these orphans knew came from Tara.

As if she read his thoughts Tara asked:

"How can I leave them, Sir? Surely there is someone else you could take?"

"I assure you that Mrs. Barrowfield said the same thing," Mr. Falkirk answered, "but she could think of no-one of the right age."

Tara drew in her breath.

"Why should His Grace want me?"

Mr. Falkirk did not answer and she said quickly:

"There is Belgrave. She was called that because she was found on a door-step in that Square. She will be eleven next year and is a big girl for her age. Would she not do?"

"I am afraid not."

"You are sure, Sir? I have taught her how to scrub a floor and although she cannot sew well she is learning."

"I am afraid she is too young."

"If only you had come last month, there was May. She would have suited you. She was past twelve but nearly as tall as I am. A good worker and a nice, cheerful girl. She would never complain, however hungry she was."

"But May is not here now and anyway she would have

been too young," Mr. Falkirk said. "I think, Tara, you would find it very interesting to visit Scotland."

He saw the firmness of his tone had brought an expression of despair to Tara's blue eyes.

"When do you want me to . . . leave, Sir?"

"This afternoon. I will call for you at about a quarter-to-three."

"Oh, Sir . . . !"

There was a wealth of meaning in the exclamation that was even more touching than if she had expressed herself in a thousand words.

Then in a low voice he could hardly hear she asked:

"I cannot . . . refuse . . . can I?"

"No, Tara. This Orphanage belongs to His Grace the Duke of Arkcraig. If he asks for one of the orphans, whoever it may be, there is no possibility of anyone, from Mrs. Barrowfield downwards, refusing to obey his request."

Tara gave a deep sigh which seemed to come from the very depths of her being.

"I will be ready, Sir," she said quietly. He admired the courage and perhaps the pride which would not let her protest any further.

He turned and went from the room and as he pulled the door to behind him he heard the children's voices break out with the cry:

"A story! A story! Yer promised us a story!"

Mr. Falkirk walked carefully down the stairs, feeling that the condition they were in might not support his weight.

He however reached the hall in safety. Picking up his hat and throwing his cloak round his shoulders he turned resolutely towards the front door.

He had no desire to argue any further with Mrs. Barrowfield. He also had the suspicion she would not be able to say very much and more than likely would be asleep.

He let himself out, then when he reached the street he turned to look back at the Orphanage.

There was no doubt it was in bad repair: the frames round the windows were almost devoid of paint, the front door was a disgrace, the knocker almost black from lack of polish.

"Duchess Anne would have been appalled!" he told himself and was determined to set things right as soon as he had permission from the Duke.

* * *

It took Tara half-an-hour to finish the story-telling, as there was not one, but three to which the children listened to attentively.

When she had finished she rose from the stool to say:

"Now that is all. Tidy things up."

"Another! Another! Tara, tell us another!"

There were a dozen small voices saying the same thing but she shook her head resolutely.

"I have to go and cook you something for dinner," she said, "or we will all be hungry."

"I'm hungry now!" one of the small girls said plaintively.

"So am I! So am I!"

The voices shouted in unison and, hurriedly in case they should hang on to her to prevent her leaving, Tara went from the dormitory and ran down the stairs.

The noise in the lower room where the older children played was deafening.

She was sure that two of the bigger boys were fighting each other.

They were always doing it and there was little she could say or do to stop them. In any case this morning she had no time.

She knocked on the door of Mrs. Barrowfield's Sitting-Room and when there was no answer, went in.

Mrs. Barrowfield, as Mr. Falkirk had anticipated, was fast asleep.

The room was very hot and airless, for however warm the weather might be Mrs. Barrowfield always insisted on a fire in her Sitting-Room.

It was to her, Tara knew, a kind of symbol, a comfort which only she could have and which she had no intention of doing without.

Surreptitiously, very quietly because she had no wish to

waken her, Tara opened the window a little, but when she saw the nearly empty port bottle on the table she knew it would take an effort to arouse Mrs. Barrowfield.

She looked fat and unpleasant with her crimson face, her mouth open and she was snoring. Tara merely picked up the bottle and put it back in the cupboard, then she collected the glasses.

As she did so she saw the trinket-box lying on the table and without being told knew that the man who was taking her to Scotland had seen the locket which had belonged to her mother.

It was the only thing, she told herself, that she really possessed, the only thing which made her different from the other thirty-nine nameless orphans who had no origin or background and nothing to identify them except the natural characteristics of hair, eyes and skin.

'I hope he will not lose it,' Tara thought anxiously.

Then she put the trinket-box back where it belonged and carrying the two dirty glasses in her hand went from the Sitting-Room shutting the door quietly behind her.

In the kitchen was one of the ancient women who came to help. She was toothless and had lost the sight of one eye, but she called herself a cook and Mrs. Barrowfield accepted her as such.

The soup which she was stirring in a huge cauldron over the fire smelt unpleasant and Tara thought it was likely to taste even worse.

But it was better than no food at all and the soup which the children had at midday was their only sustaining meal.

There was however, thank goodness, bread and that was supplied to the Orphanage only because Tara had insisted on Mrs. Barrowfield paying the baker last week and giving him a little in advance.

Only she was aware of how much money which was allotted for the use of the orphans went in the drink which kept Mrs. Barrowfield content and comfortable, if no-one else was.

Tara did not worry herself unduly about it, except when

26

the children were ill from lack of food or so hungry that they could not sleep at night.

It was then she would fight fiercely with Mrs. Barrowfield for their rights.

Because the older woman was too indolent to oppose her for long she invariably capitulated and handed over some of the precious money she had been intending to keep for herself.

Tara cut up the loaves into equal slices knowing as she did so that if she was not watchful the bigger boys would take the younger ones' share away from them.

They would also toady to the girls, hoping that by doing so they would be generous enough to offer them part of their ration.

It was only Tara who kept the Orphanage from falling under the rule of the strongest boys and the biggest bullies.

She never used violence against the children as Mrs. Barrowfield was occasionally galvanised into doing. She kept them in order by sheer force of personality.

This had evolved simply because she had no alternative but to build up a mental dominance where a physical one would have been impossible.

Having finished cutting the bread she saw out of the corner of her eye the old woman hurriedly secreting something in the corner of the kitchen.

She knew only too well what was taking place, and she walked across to reach over her blind shoulder and take away from her what she was hiding under her threadbare, dilapidated coat.

It was a large hunk of meat – cheap meat it was true – but all they could afford. It should have been the foundation of the soup the so-called cook had been stirring on the hearth for the last hour.

The old woman gave a scream of fury but Tara ignored her.

She merely put the meat on the table and started to cut it up into the smallest possible pieces, chopping and re-chopping until they were little more than mince.

27

"It's mine!"

The old woman almost spat the words at her.

"That is untrue, Mary, as you well know," Tara said. "The children are hungry. They have to have something to eat or they will die."

"And a good job too, if ye asks me! Who wants 'em?"

This was an unanswerable question which Tara had often asked herself.

"You must not be greedy, Mary," she said quietly. "It would be unfortunate, as you well know, if the children died because you had stolen their food."

"I'se hungry at night when Oi gets home," Mary said in a whining voice, "and me poor cats has never a bite to eat."

"They can catch mice," Tara retorted, "but the children here cannot do that any more than they can go out and pick an apple from a tree."

She gave a sigh.

"Oh, Mary, I wish the Orphanage was in the country. I am sure it would be much easier than living here in London."

"London's all right when ye've got money," Mary said in a surly tone.

"I suppose everywhere is all right in that case," Tara answered.

She finished chopping the meat and picking it up in her hands she put it into the boiling cauldron of soup, stirring it in until a very different aroma filled the air.

She added some salt, saw a few small onions had been left on the table and added them too.

"Go on stirring, Mary," she said, "and I will call the children. Have you washed their bowls?"

Mary did not answer, which told Tara she had not done so and did not intend to.

It was always the same, she thought with a sigh. One could never rely on Mary for a moment and the other old woman who came in the afternoons and was supposed to clean the floor was even worse.

Because the Orphanage was so full there was no Dining-Room.

It had been converted into another dormitory with a few beds and mattresses on the floor. So the children had to eat standing up in the Hall or sitting on the stairs.

This made it difficult for Tara to see that everyone had a fair share of whatever food was available.

She rang the bell and at the sound of it the doors opened and like a tidal wave the children came tearing into the kitchen from all directions.

Only the babies were left behind upstairs and Tara knew she must keep a sharp look out for the pail of milk in a corner of the kitchen.

Otherwise when her back was turned there would be a number of cups and spoons dipped into it by the children who were considered to be too old to require milk.

The conduct of the next five minutes was like repelling a storm at sea from breaking up the ship.

"No, only one piece of bread each! Fred, put that down immediately, you have had your share. Careful, Helen, or you will upset your soup. Do not push each other, there is plenty for everyone if you wait."

These were the same remarks she made every day at every meal-time.

It was not because they did not love her that they disobeyed and tried to cheat and steal from each other, but simply because the animal instinct of self-preservation told them they must eat or die.

She ladled the last teaspoonful of soup from the cauldron and found a small boy snatching up the last piece of bread from the last loaf on the kitchen table.

That meant there was nothing left for herself but she accepted it, as she had accepted it a hundred times with resignation.

'It is my own fault,' she thought. 'I should remember to eat my piece of bread before I call the children.'

She had learnt the hard way that to go without food for too long was to become so weak and faint that she was in danger of dropping the babies and the thought of that frightened her.

There was still a chance of being offered a cup of tea. It

was a luxury Mrs. Barrowfield kept entirely for herself but if she was in a good temper Tara was sometimes allowed the dregs of the pot.

There were two large pork chops that Mary had cooked for her employer, put neatly on a clean plate, and beside it a couple of fried onions.

"Here's her Nibs' tea," Mary said plonking the tea-pot down on the tray and rattling the cup and saucer as she did so.

"Thank you, Mary, but you have forgotten the potatoes."

There had been a number of potatoes in the soup, many of them beginning to go bad because it was cheaper to buy throw-outs, but three perfect ones, large and fluffy, were set down beside the chops and despite herself Tara felt her mouth watering.

"Perhaps the gentleman will give me something to eat to-night," she told herself hopefully as she carried the tray into Mrs. Barrowfield's Sitting-Room.

Chapter Two

Tara leaned forward in the coach to exclaim:

"It is so green! I knew that the countryside would be green, but not as green as this!"

Mr. Falkirk was just about to reply when she said in a tone of rapture:

"And that field is gold – really gold!"

"Corn," Mr. Falkirk remarked laconically, then asked:

"Surely you have been in the country before?"

Tara shook her head.

"No. Mrs. Barrowfield allowed me to take the older children into Hyde Park, but lately there have been too many little ones to look after and she could not spare me."

"The children must have gone out," Mr. Falkirk protested.

"They played on the ground behind the Orphanage," Tara replied. "It is quite small and very muddy in the winter, but at least they were in the fresh air."

She turned her face towards him while she answered the question, but now once again she bent forward and looked out of the window.

"If only the children could see this," she said beneath her breath.

Mr. Falkirk had already realised that her thoughts were seldom away from the children she had left behind her.

There had been an emotional scene which he had found strangely moving when he collected Tara from the Orphanage.

The smaller children had clung to her crying and wailing, and the older ones had shouted almost despairingly until the carriage was out of sight.

Even Mrs. Barrowfield had appeared to be sentimental at

the thought of losing Tara, but Mr. Falkirk could not help thinking her sorrow was more for herself because she would be without an able assistant.

But for whatever reason it was obviously very difficult for Tara to say good-bye.

When finally she disentangled herself from the clinging arms of the younger children and joined Mr. Falkirk in the coach, the tears were streaming down her cheeks.

It took her some time to gain control of herself, and only when they had driven for some minutes did she manage to say:

"Wh . what will the ... ch . children do without me? I am ... sure the younger ones will g . go hungry."

"That is what I was going to tell you, Tara," Mr. Falkirk answered. "I have realised that the children are not having enough to eat and the whole Orphanage has fallen into a lamentable state of disrepair which should never have been allowed."

He saw that Tara was looking at him with a desperate look of anxiety in her wet eyes, and he said quickly because he did not wish her to go on suffering:

"I have made arrangements which I feel sure will meet with your approval."

"Wh . what are ... they?" Tara asked, her voice catching in a little sob.

"The Housekeeper at Arkcraig House is an elderly woman but a very capable one. She remembers when she was young the Orphanage being built and she also served Duchess Anne and knew the personal interest she took in the orphans."

"It was only after Her Grace died that things got so bad," Tara said.

"That is what I realised," Mr. Falkirk answered. "I have told Mrs. Kingston to engage a Cook who will buy adequate food for the children."

The expression of joy on Tara's thin face seemed to transform it.

Mr. Falkirk knew he had been right in thinking that most of the money which had been paid to the Orphanage weekly by the Duke's Solicitors had been spent by Mrs. Barrowfield on drink.

"Mrs. Kingston will also find some young girls who will clean the place," he went on, "and help in looking after the children."

He paused, then said almost sharply:

"What I cannot understand is what happened to the teachers. There were, I know, quite a number of them in the Duchess Anne's time."

"Two of them retired and they were not replaced," Tara answered, "and the last one left about six months ago when she found she could not control the older boys."

She paused and in almost a pleading tone said:

"It is not that they are so naughty, but she did not teach very well."

She looked at Mr. Falkirk apprehensively as if she thought he would be angry and added:

"I have been teaching the younger ones myself when I had time, but when there were babies to care for it was very difficult."

"And so you told them stories," Mr. Falkirk said with a smile. "I am sure they preferred that."

"That is why I made the stories a treat," Tara explained, "and it kept them quiet."

"I am sure it did," he said. "But I shall speak to His Grace and make sure that proper teachers are appointed to the Orphanage as there used to be in the past."

"That will be wonderful!" Tara cried. "Oh, dear, I wish I could be there. There is so much I want to learn."

Mr. Falkirk looked at her with a smile and said:

"I am sure you must have had quite a lot of lessons in your time?"

"Not enough," Tara replied. "The Minister was very kind to me but he died last year."

There was a note in her voice which told Mr. Falkirk that the Minister's death had been a loss which still hurt her.

"Where did the Minister come from?" he enquired.

"From the Presbyterian Church in Chelsea," Tara answered. "I think perhaps it is the only one in London."

"And he held services in the Orphanage?"

"Every Sunday, but he also came two or three times a week to instruct us all in the Scriptures."

She gave a little sigh.

"His lessons were so interesting. I used to look forward to them more than to anything else, and he lent me books."

"So you can read fluently."

"I love reading!" Tara replied, "but when the Minister died I had only the Bible that he had given me."

She looked at Mr. Falkirk with a shy smile and added:

"I think sometimes I must know it by heart."

That would account for the extremely good English she spoke, Mr. Falkirk thought.

He had noticed already what a cultured way she had of speaking and that her vocabulary was far greater than he would have expected from a child brought up in an Orphanage.

"His Grace has a very large Library at the Castle," he told her.

He saw the look of excitement in Tara's eyes. Then it was dimmed as she said:

"I do not expect His Grace would allow me to ... touch his books."

"I am quite certain he would lend them to you if you were careful," Mr. Falkirk answered. "And if not, I have a considerable collection myself to which you are very welcome."

"Do you really mean that, Sir?"

He was amused by the manner in which she spoke which was one of awe and excitement.

"I actually have some books with me now," he said. "When we stop to-night I will unpack them and you can choose what would interest you to read on the journey. I am afraid though, you may find them rather heavy and dull."

"I would find nothing I could read dull," Tara replied. "I long to read and have longed to have enough money to buy a newspaper. But Mrs. Barrowfield always said we could not afford to buy one."

Mr. Falkirk's lips tightened.

He had already made up his mind that he would urge the Duke to pension off Mrs. Barrowfield and put a sensible, motherly woman in her place.

Someone must be found who would not only care for the children but prepare them for the world outside into which the majority of the orphans were precipitated at the age of twelve.

One thing however that had worried him more than anything else was the obvious lack of food and decent clothing at the Orphanage.

He looked at Tara now and was relieved to find that her grey dress with its white collar was not only clean but also in a fairly good state of repair.

He thought it was an ugly uniform and the severity of it, especially the tight helmet-shaped cap, was what might have been expected to be the choice of Duchess Harriet.

The Founder of The Orphanage of the Nameless had been an austere Scotswoman who could be colloquially described as "having no frills about her".

He thought that Tara might in fact be quite attractive if she was not so pitiably thin and the bones of her wrists when they protruded from the black cloth cloak in which she was travelling were not so distressingly prominent.

"I am going to make a bargain with you," he said aloud.

"A bargain?"

"Yes, I will lend you my books on condition that you eat everything that is put in front of you until we reach Scotland."

Tara gave a little laugh.

"You will not find me saying no, Sir, to any food you offer me."

But that, Mr. Falkirk was to find, was an optimistic aspiration she could not fulfil.

When they stopped at the first Posting Inn at Baldock where they were to stay the night, Tara found the bed-room she had been allotted upstairs exceeded all her imaginings of comfort and luxury.

She washed her hands and face, changed into another

35

grey cotton gown which was identical to the one she had been wearing and went downstairs to join Mr. Falkirk.

She guessed that he would change for supper from something he had said when they had arrived at the Inn and only some of their luggage had been lifted down from the top of the coach.

But she was not prepared for the difference his evening dress made and she stared in wide-eyed astonishment at the elegance of his cut-away coat with long tails and the crisp muslin cravat at his throat.

But her admiration for Mr. Falkirk was superseded by her astonishment at the amount of food which was being carried into the Sitting-Room by the Landlord and two mob-capped maids.

There were hot dishes of mulligatawny soup, a leg of mutton and two plump pigeons roasted on a spit.

There was also a side-table groaning with cold meats, a lark and oyster pie, a loin of pork, a brawn which the Landlord warmly recommended, several plump chickens and a large ham.

"I feel you must be hungry, Tara, as I am," Mr. Falkirk said as they sat down at the table.

He noticed with approval that she waited to see which spoon he chose for the soup before she began to drink her own.

Once she started she ate quickly and he had a feeling that she was controlling herself or else she would have eaten more quickly still.

As soon as they finished the soup the Landlord came in with a fine turbot which he apologised for not bringing earlier but explained that his wife had only just cooked it "to a turn".

"I know you will find this to your liking, Sir," he said to Mr. Falkirk, "and the little lady will enjoy it, too."

Mr. Falkirk noticed that Tara only helped herself to a bare spoonful of the fish and thought that the glance she gave him was a question as to whether she was taking too much.

He however said nothing and when it came to carving the leg of mutton he helped her liberally.

Only as he finished his own plate did he realise that she had eaten little more than a quarter of what he had given her.

"You do not like the mutton?" he enquired.

"It seems very ungrateful, Sir, but I just cannot eat any more."

She gave a little sigh and added:

"If only we could send some of this food back to the Orphanage."

"I am not concerned with the Orphanage at the moment," Mr. Falkirk replied, "but with you, Tara. You promised me you would eat everything that was put in front of you."

"I know, Sir, but it is impossible ... it is really. I feel so full that I could not eat another mouthful."

"What had you eaten already to-day?"

There was silence for a moment, then he said:

"I want to know."

"I had a ... piece of bread and ... dripping for breakfast, Sir," Tara said. "But there ... was not enough for everyone at ... dinner-time."

"I have promised you that is something that will be remedied in the future," Mr. Falkirk said, "so I want you to eat sensibly. It will not benefit the children you have left behind if you go on starving yourself because you are thinking of them and make no effort to get strong, as I know His Grace would want you to be."

"I will ... try ... I really will try," Tara promised.

Because Mr. Falkirk pressed her, she managed to eat a few spoonfuls of the Port Wine jelly which the Landlord said was one of the specialities of the Inn.

Mr. Falkirk on the other hand did full justice to the menu which he assured Tara was very much better than they would find in some of the other Inns where they would stay on the way to Scotland.

He also drank a bottle of expensive claret but he did not offer Tara any.

They set off again early the next morning and although she was very quiet at first because she had no desire to be obtrusive or in any way a nuisance to him, Mr. Falkirk soon discovered that she was in fact bursting with questions.

He found it rather fascinating to find himself seeing the countryside through the eyes of a girl who for nearly eighteen years had been virtually imprisoned in one building with little or no contact with the world outside.

As they journeyed on he was surprised not only by Tara's intelligence but also that through the reading she had done and her imagination her mind was developed to an extent he had not expected.

It amused him to see her reaction to new situations and to find out what she thought about people both rich and poor.

"It seems strange," she said in the course of one conversation, "that there should be so many very rich people living in London and that they should not care in any way about the very, very poor."

"Do you mean the people you see in the streets?" Mr. Falkirk asked.

"Yes, Sir, the crossing-sweepers, the poor old women like Mary, who although she is too old, works at the Orphanage because otherwise she would starve to death. Surely someone ought to look after them?"

"I have often thought that myself," Mr. Falkirk admitted.

"And the children, they suffer and no-one seems to care. The doctor says often enough that if we did not take a child in it would either die of neglect, or someone would throw it into the river just to be rid of it!"

There was a note of pain in Tara's voice when she spoke of such things which made Mr. Falkirk realise she was very sensitive – unusually so for a girl of her upbringing.

"If I were rich," she was saying, "and sometimes I pretend I have come into millions and millions of pounds, I would have proper schools where all the children would go and not have to pay a penny for it."

"Do you think they would enjoy that?"

"If they are educated they have a chance of getting better jobs," Tara replied. "The men who come to the Orphanage for apprentices always ask if a boy can read or write. With the girls it is not so important."

"So you think all children should learn to read?"

"There is nothing more wonderful than reading a book."

Mr. Falkirk smiled.

"I think you will find there are other things which will interest you – things you can do and things you can see as well as reading about them."

There was silence for a moment. Then Tara asked:

"What will His Grace want me to do? Do you think there are children for me to look after?"

"I have no idea," Mr. Falkirk answered, "and that is the truth, Tara. His Grace told me to bring a girl from the Orphanage with me to Scotland, and I had to obey his instructions."

"Mrs. Barrowfield said that you were His Grace's Comptroller."

"And so I am," Mr. Falkirk agreed. "I was Comptroller to the last Duke until he died, and now I am Comptroller to his son, the 5th Duke of Arkcraig."

"And is there a Duchess?"

"There was, but she died recently."

"And she had no children? I thought perhaps that was why you were taking me to Scotland. I would like to look after children."

"I am afraid there are no children at Arkcraig Castle," Mr. Falkirk said, "although there are plenty on the Estate."

"Then perhaps I shall be in the laundry," Tara mused. "I am quite good at washing – when I have the soap."

Mr. Falkirk did not reply and after a moment she went on:

"I would rather not be in the kitchen, but I do not suppose I shall be given the choice. I must do as His Grace tells me."

"That is what we all have to do," Mr. Falkirk said in a somewhat overhearty manner.

He was finding that Tara's puzzled questioning about the reason she was being taken to Scotland only increased his own irritation at the fact that the Duke had not confided in him.

Because he supposed they had both been on edge and deeply disturbed by what had taken place in France he had not pressed his employer as he might otherwise have done to be more explicit.

The Duke had merely given him an order to bring a girl from the Orphanage with him to Scotland and had set off almost immediately in the travelling carriage which was waiting at the door.

There had been four out-riders to escort him, and behind there had been a landau which conveyed his luggage, his valet and a secretary whom Mr. Falkirk had to instruct at the last moment to see to the payment of bills at the hostelries where His Grace would be staying.

He had in fact been so astounded at being left behind and not to be travelling in the usual cavalcade with which the Duke moved about the country, that it was only when the landau had disappeared out of sight that he realised there were a dozen questions that remained unanswered.

Now he found himself wondering if in fact he had misinterpreted the Duke's requirements.

But His Grace had been very explicit and there had been a conciseness about his orders which made them quite impossible to be misunderstood.

It had certainly been tactful, Mr. Falkirk told himself, to say as little as possible to the Duke at that particular moment when he had obviously passed a sleepless night and the dark lines under his eyes were only echoed by the scowl between them.

He had obviously not wished to talk and Mr. Falkirk, although he would have liked to express his sympathy and understanding, had realised the kindest thing he could do was to say nothing and intrude as little as possible on his employer.

It was however not only difficult, but in fact impossible not to worry as the miles sped by about what would be awaiting both him and Tara when they arrived in Scotland.

There was however a very long journey ahead of them and Mr. Falkirk could only be grateful that at this time of the year the roads were dry and there was no question of their being bogged down in mud or lost in a fog such as he had experienced on other occasions when travelling to and from the North.

The weather was bright and sunny, and despite the fact that it was June not so hot as to make them feel overcome by the heat.

There was always a faint, fresh breeze coming through the open windows.

At first Mr. Falkirk had felt slightly concerned that the Duke had taken all the out-riders with him and left the second coach in which he and Tara travelled without any protection against Highwaymen or Foot-pads.

But it was a relief to know that the only dust which was thrown up was by the wheels of their coach.

Despite Tara's excitement, having once lost her shyness and her stream of questions, Mr. Falkirk slept a great deal of the way.

He knew that as soon as his eyes closed Tara would open one of the books he had lent her and curling up in the corner of the carriage would read and go on reading until he opened his eyes again.

He was so interested in her reactions to the rather heavy political books which were in his luggage and also to the latest commentary on the Rebellion of '45 that Mr. Falkirk found himself sitting up later in the evening than he intended.

He not only talked over with Tara what she had read but told her his own ideas on the subjects discussed in the books and on a great many other matters as well.

It was only when finally he was alone in his own bedroom that he realised almost in consternation that he had been lecturing, arguing and conversing with Tara as if she had been a contemporary.

She should actually, he told himself, be wondering on what work she might be expected to do at the Castle rather than filling her mind with subjects which could never concern her in her limited life.

"The girl is exceptional – there is no doubt about that, and it is a pity . . ."

He checked himself, realising that to show himself too sympathetic towards Tara would undoubtedly prejudice her in the eyes of other servants.

She would be in a difficult and indeed unpleasant position from the very outset because she was illegitimate.

However loose-minded London might have become, and there was no doubt that the Regency had set a deplorable standard where morals were concerned, the Scottish were still extremely puritanical and strait-laced.

Because she had no father Tara would be branded as an undesirable person and that she was a Sassenach would make it worse.

"The best thing I could do for her would be to send her back," Mr. Falkirk said aloud.

He began to blame himself for having carried out the Duke's orders so punctiliously.

It would have been quite easy if instead of taking Tara to Scotland he had returned empty-handed and informed His Grace that since there was no orphaned girl of the right age, there had been nothing he could do about it.

It would have been a lie, or perhaps he could have called it more kindly an evasion of the truth, for the simple reason that Tara was no ordinary orphan.

It must have escaped His Grace's memory that the orphans were in fact apprenticed at the age of twelve.

"It was stupid of me not to have thought of that before," Mr. Falkirk told himself not once but a dozen times on the succeeding days.

But now there was nothing he could do and as the coach moved relentlessly on through the north of England towards the Scottish border he was finding Tara more and more interesting and therefore became more and more afraid of what awaited her at Arkcraig Castle.

He knew quite dispassionately that she was exceptional, and that he might have picked up a thousand orphans on the Duke's instructions and not found one to equal her.

On the second day of their journey just before they arrived at the Posting Inn where they were to stay the night Tara had said a little hesitatingly :

"May I ... ask you a ... favour, Sir?"

"But of course," Mr. Falkirk replied. "What is it?"

"I realise how very ... ignorant I am as to how I should ... behave or what I should do," Tara replied, "and as I do not wish to make ... mistakes I should be grateful if you would ... instruct and correct me."

She looked at him anxiously as she said:

"I will not be a ... nuisance or a bother to you, Sir, but I have always longed to behave as a lady would when she sits at ... table or indeed whatever she is doing ... but I have never found a book on the subject."

"I believe there are such books," Mr. Falkirk said, "but may I say, Tara, that I think you have an instinct for what is right which is more important than anything you can read in a book."

"You are very kind, Sir," Tara answered, "but I well know I do a dozen things wrong. I have tried to copy the way you hold your knife and fork which is different to the way in which Mrs. Barrowfield holds hers."

"That is to be expected," Mr. Falkirk said with a smile, "and I will show you the right way, Tara."

But he wondered what good it would do her while he taught her not only how to eat and how to handle her knives and forks, but also how to lift her cup to her lips and how to sit gracefully on a chair.

As she would spend the rest of her life amongst servants who mostly behaved in exactly the opposite way to what was considered correct by their employers, he only hoped she would not be jeered at and laughed at because she was different.

"But then she *is* different," he told himself and wished once again that he had left her where she was, although he wondered how long she could have survived such an existence.

There was no doubt that despite the tiring journey there was already an improvement in her appearance even after one week.

The tension had gone from her face, and he thought that her chin was no longer so sharply etched or the skin so tight over her bones as it had been when he first saw her.

She was also putting on a little weight, for Tara had told him that her waist-band was so tight that she had to sit up at night letting out her skirts because they were uncomfortable.

"I am hoping that when we get to Scotland you will make yourself an entirely new gown," Mr. Falkirk had said.

Tara had looked at him and he knew before she spoke what she was going to ask.

"Do you think I shall have to ... wear these clothes when I am at the Castle?" she questioned in a low voice, "or will I be able to dress like other people?"

"I think that is another question for His Grace."

"He decides everything, does he not?"

"Yes, he does," Mr. Falkirk agreed. "You see, Tara, although English aristocrats have a great deal of power and importance, the Duke of Arkcraig is in a category all of his own."

"Why is that?"

"Because he is in the position not only of being a nobleman but also the Chieftain of his Clan."

"I am reading about the Clans in one of your books."

"And I think you will find there are a great many references to the McCraigs," Mr. Falkirk said. "They are part of the history of Scotland and fought in all the great battles in which Scotland was involved."

"Stirling Bridge for one," Tara said.

"Of course," Mr. Falkirk agreed, "and the battle which took place in 1298 – do you know what that was?"

She thought for a moment.

"I read about it last night ... yes, of course! It had the same name as you ... the Battle of Falkirk!"

"That is right!"

"I was thinking what a brave man Wallace was," Tara said. "Yet he was hanged, drawn and quartered."

"King Edward could never forget that he devastated Northumberland and won at Stirling Bridge," Mr. Falkirk said.

"Your books speak as if battles were fine and glorious,

but I kept thinking of the men who were wounded, and how there would be no-one to look after them."

"That is true. And if they were not killed in battle the majority of them died of any wound they might have received. It was a harsh age, but to-day the Clans have ceased fighting, they grow their crops and tend their cattle in peace."

"And do they still look to their Chieftain to guide them?"

"They believe in him, they trust him. Without a Chieftain the Clan is like a ship without a rudder or a sheep without a shepherd."

Mr. Falkirk spoke almost harshly.

He was thinking of how some of the Highland Chieftains had been beguiled into seeking the amusements and the gaieties of the South and had left Scotland for the glamour of the Hanoverian Court in London.

In consequence their Clans became dispersed, many of them being exploited by Lowlanders in search of cheap labour.

Others were being transported overseas by those who planned to turn the Highlands into a vast sheep-walk and were clearing the moors of the people who had lived there for centuries.

He had forgotten Tara for the moment until he heard her ask:

"Will you tell me, Sir, about the present Duke? Is he a young man?"

"His Grace has just turned thirty," Mr. Falkirk answered. "He is exceedingly handsome and, I am sure you will think, looks exactly as a Chieftain should."

He paused before he said diffidently:

"But His Grace has had troubles lately and I can only pray that the future will prove fairer for him than the past has been."

Tara looked interested, but she was perceptive enough to realise since Mr. Falkirk changed the subject that he had no wish to dissertate further upon the subject of his employer.

Because there were so many other things she wanted to

ask, it was not until they were within a day's drive of Arkcraig Castle that the Duke seemed suddenly to overshadow
her mind until the thought of him created an apprehension
that made her unaccountably nervous.

"We are now on McCraig territory," Mr. Falkirk had informed her the previous day.

Tara had seen women with baskets on their heads selling
little bunches of Scotch heather in the streets of London,
mostly white, but also some purple.

However it now looked very different on the great moors,
vividly purple with the heather coming into bloom.

The light on the hills seemed to her to have a fairylike
quality that was echoed by the blue lochs and the mists
which hid them in the mornings.

Never had she imagined there could be such an enchanted
land of light and shade, with colours that were so brilliant
they seemed unreal, with skies that changed from blue to
grey and from sunshine to rain as if they were as tempera-
mental as any woman.

"Is it what you expected?" Mr. Falkirk asked.

"It is like nothing I ever dreamt existed," Tara breathed.
"It is beautiful ... so beautiful that it hurts me to look at it."

He understood what she was trying to say and he understood too why her books were forgotten and she sat at the
window all day with the wind blowing the fragrance of the
heather in her face.

At times she seemed spellbound until her eyes were as
full of mystery as the silver cascades and the burns running crystal clear beside the roadway.

If Tara was nervous as to what lay ahead, Mr. Falkirk
was also apprehensive.

He knew that during the journey he had been instruc-
mental in changing Tara in many ways from the girl he
had taken from the Orphanage.

It was not only the instructions he had given her, the
things he had explained, his answers to her questions which
had made a difference.

It was also the manner in which they were travelling together, which was not only different from the way she had

lived in the past but would in fact also be very different from the way she would live in the future.

"Perhaps she should have travelled as a servant," Mr. Falkirk told himself.

In which case he should either have insisted on another landau coming behind them or have made her sit up on the box squeezed between the coachman and the footman as being her rightful place.

Instead, really without thinking about it, he had taken her with him as if she were a well-born young woman of his acquaintance.

In the Posting Inns she had slept in the best rooms, she had eaten with him in a private parlour, and she had been waited on by the maids and spoken to politely by the men-servants.

Because she was receptive, sensitive and had an instinct for what was right and wrong, Tara was behaving on the journey in the same manner that any Lady of Quality would have done. She was only betrayed by the clothes she wore.

"It has been a mistake – I am afraid it has been a mistake," Mr. Falkirk said aloud, and yet he knew that if he had the choice again, he would still have behaved in exactly the same manner.

Childless and, although he had loved many women, having never taken one for a wife, Mr. Falkirk found it fascinating to watch a bud open and become a flower which he could not help thinking was of a surprising beauty.

There was something in Tara's mind that responded to his, and he knew she was the type of pupil that every teacher dreamt of finding.

One so mentally alert, so receptive, that it was not only what he said that she assimilated but what he thought.

"God knows what will happen to her," he told himself, and he knew that if he obeyed his inclination he would send her back to London now and at once before they reached the Castle.

Unaware of what he was thinking Tara was staring up at the mountains peaking above them and leaning forward to catch a glimpse of a silver cascade falling down the grey

47

barren side of rock into a loch that lay at its foot.

"It is more beautiful every time I look out of the window," she said. "There is something about Scotland that makes me feel ... although you may think it ridiculous ... that I belong here, that it is a part of me ... a part of my heart."

* * *

Two carriages moving up the tree-bordered drive towards the Castle contained six men wearing the green and yellow check tartan of the Kildonnons.

The Chief of the Clan, a fine-looking man, his bristling side-whiskers echoed by heavy eyebrows and a greying moustache, lay back at his ease.

But his brother and his two sons, also wearing the tartan, were still discussing amongst themselves the reason for their being invited to the Castle.

"Why do you think, father, that the Duke has sent for us in such a peremptory manner?"

"It was an order more than an invitation," his other son said.

"That is true enough," their uncle agreed. "It was not a question of: 'Will you come?' It was: 'Be at the Castle at four o'clock on the 10th July, whether you like it or not'!"

"I dare say the Duke wishes to describe to us his visit to France," The Kildonnon said.

His title was one of the oldest in Scotland, for although the Kildonnons were a small Clan they had a long history and were intensely proud.

"You knew he had been to France?" the Chief's brother enquired.

"Yes, I knew that."

"And you do not think perhaps there was some special reason for him going there?"

There was a silence after the question had been asked, and it was a moment before The Kildonnon enquired:

"What do you mean by that?"

There was again silence, except for the noise of wheels and the horses' hoofs before Alister Kildonnon replied:

"There have been rumours – although I do not know

whether you have heard them — that Margaret went to France a month or so ago."

"Margaret went to France?" The Kildonnon echoed. "Who says so? Why was I not told of it?"

"I am not sure that it is true," his brother answered. "All I heard was that she had left the Castle and gone South."

The two sons of The Kildonnon sitting on the seats opposite exchanged glances.

It was obvious they could have said something if they wished to, but as if by some secret signal each tightened his lips and sat in silence.

They were fine-looking young men, one of nineteen and one of twenty-three.

They wore their bonnets at a rakish angle and when they walked it was with a swagger which was emulated by a great many of the young men of the Kildonnon Clan.

"Well, we shall know whether or not Margaret is in France when we reach the Castle," Alister Kildonnon said as the horses took the strain of the last uprise of the drive.

Arkcraig Castle was situated high above the valley in a magnificent position that had been chosen centuries ago when the McCraigs fortified their stronghold against the onslaughts of their enemies.

The most aggressive of these were the Kildonnons.

The feud that existed between the two Clans in their constant warfaring had left its toll in the shape of in-numerable graves in the Churchyard lower down the hill.

Above the Castle with its battlements, its towers, its arrow-slits in the Keep, the outer wall of what had once been an impregnable fortification, rose high hills which in the winter were always white with snow.

But now the heather was coming into full bloom making a striking background for the grey stone.

The horses drew up with a flourish outside the huge door-way which was decorated with brass-studded nails and wrought-iron hinges of great antiquity.

The moment the horses came to a standstill the door was opened and the Duke's servants, all wearing the tartan of the McCraigs and sporrans of badgers' fur, were waiting to usher in the guests.

A second carriage contained the two sons, who were twins, of The Kildonnon's brother Alister.

The six clansmen were led with some ceremony by a Major Domo wearing a more resplendent sporran than the other servants up the broad stairs to the first floor.

There were situated, as was usual in Scotland, the main Reception Rooms, the largest and most important of them being the Chief's Room where the Kildonnons knew the Duke would receive them.

It was a magnificent room with high windows overlooking the gardens below the Castle and beyond them the grey loch surrounded by the undulating moorland where both stags and grouse abounded.

There was no-one to receive them in the Chief's room, and The Kildonnon walked to the window to look out enviously both at the loch which he knew was full of fresh-run salmon and also at the moors which were better than his own and certainly carried more deer.

He had however not come either to admire or to envy another Chieftain's possessions.

Although he was not prepared to admit it, he was asking the same question that the others had asked — why had they been commanded by the Duke to come to the Castle and had the rumours concerning the Duchess any foundation in fact?

The door at the far end of the Chief's room opened and through it came the Duke of Arkcraig.

One glance at him was enough to tell The Kildonnon this was no friendly meeting but a formal occasion, although why and for what reason he had no idea.

The Duke of Arkcraig was tall — taller than any of the Kildonnons — and to-day he held himself stiffly and they had only to look at his face to know that something was very much amiss.

In the last year since the Duke had become his son-in-law The Kildonnon had grown to know and like him and usually there was no formality about their meetings.

The Duke would greet him with an eager hand-shake and at once plunge into a discussion over their joint interests which invariably concerned their Clans.

But to-day the Duke, having advanced towards them, stood for a moment staring at The Kildonnon as if he had never seen him before.

There was a scowl on his face that was unmistakable and a darkness in his eyes which was a portent of anger that made the clansmen feel as if they were arrested where they stood.

As if he had meant to be impressive the Duke was wearing the full regalia of a Chieftain, his white sporran ornamented with silver hung over his red, blue and white tartan, his plaid was fastened on the shoulder with a huge cairngorm brooch. There was lace at his throat and his skeandhu glinted in his diced hose.

The silence in which the Duke was receiving them made The Kildonnon aware of a tension that seemed as ominous as a dark cloud over the moorland.

Then with an effort, because as an older man he felt he should speak and disperse the discomfort of which they were all aware, he said :

"Good afternoon, Arkcraig! You asked us to visit you and as you see we are all here!"

"Good afternoon!"

The Duke's voice was cold and hard.

"Will you kindly seat yourselves."

He indicated with his hand as he spoke some chairs drawn up in a row at the far end of the room.

In front of them was a high-backed elaborately carved Chieftain's chair which The Kildonnon knew was only used on formal occasions.

He was aware that his sons and nephews were exchanging glances with each other.

But because he did not wish to show any sign of the fear that was rising in him, he walked forward as the Duke suggested and seated himself, making an effort to cross his legs and appear at his ease.

The rest of the Kildonnons followed him, and only when

they were all seated did the Duke walk slowly with an air of authority that was inescapable to what seemed at this juncture to be almost a Chieftain's throne.

He did not sit down, he only stood in front of it. Then with his eyes on The Kildonnon he said slowly and distinctly:

"I have brought you here, Kildonnon, to hear the truth about your daughter Margaret, my wife the Duchess of Arkcraig, who is now dead!"

Chapter Three

"Dead!"

The word sounded like an explosion as it echoed round the Chieftain's Room.

Then as the Clansmen stared at the Duke incredulously The Kildonnon said slowly:

"Why was I not told?"

"I am telling you now!"

"And where is her body?"

"She is buried in France beside her lover."

There was an audible gasp before the Duke said harshly:

"I am ready to tell you what occurred, which is why I have brought you here."

The Kildonnon sat glaring at him, his heavy eyebrows almost meeting across his forehead.

The others were rigid in their seats and only the Duke standing in front of them seemed almost insultingly at his ease.

There was however an expression on his face so grim, so stern, that it seemed as if overnight he had changed from a young man into an old one.

The Duke addressed himself to The Kildonnon.

"When you and I agreed that our Clans would live in peace and there would be no more fighting between us, you suggested certain things I could do to bring about this enviable state of neighbourliness."

The Kildonnon nodded his head in agreement.

"Your first suggestion," the Duke went on, "was that I should grant you a loan of ten thousand pounds to help the impoverished members of your Clan and those you alleged had suffered at the hands of mine."

"That was true enough!" Alister Kildonnon interrupted. "It was the McCraigs who laid waste our crops, who had scattered our herds and stolen our sheep!"

He spoke angrily and aggressively but the Duke completely ignored the interruption. With his eyes on The Kildonnon he continued as if no one had spoken:

"Your second suggestion was that to make sure our Clans were closely allied I should marry your daughter, Margaret."

Now there was a silence which seemed to fill the whole room; a silence as if six men held their breath.

"You pointed out," the Duke continued, "that if your daughter became the Duchess of Arkcraig there was a great deal she could do to help the women of the Kildonnons. By encouraging their crafts, she would make them realise that the days of warring were over and that their children should be brought up to accept the idea of peace."

The Kildonnon did not speak and the Duke asked:

"Is not that what you suggested and to which I agreed?"

"It was," The Kildonnon replied briefly.

"Because I believed that what you and I contemplated was of great advantage not only to your Clan but to mine," the Duke continued, "I lent you the money and I also married your daughter."

For a moment he looked at the other members of the Clan, and there was something so contemptuous in his glance that they stiffened as if he had spat at them.

"I was not aware," the Duke said sternly, "that your daughter was not in agreement with your ideas and had no intention of adhering to the rosy picture of peace and prosperity we had envisaged together for the future."

He looked again at the other Kildonnons as he went on:

"She cheated, as doubtless the McCraigs would say the Kildonnons have cheated all through the centuries."

"I consider that an insult!" Alister Kildonnon cried.

"It is a fact!" the Duke retorted. "Margaret Kildonnon on the night I married her informed me that she loathed me and every member of my Clan, what is more, she would not stoop to be my wife in anything but name."

Again there was that poignant silence until The Kildonnon said in a very different tone:

"You must believe me, Arkcraig, when I tell you I had no idea she felt like that."

"I imagined that time might assuage her bitterness," the Duke answered, "but what I did not know, and what was doubtless known to certain members of your family, was that Margaret had a lover, whom she did not dismiss on her marriage."

The Kildonnon stiffened and now his sons glanced at each other and then away again as if in embarrassment.

"I am told that the husband is always the last to learn that his wife is an adultress."

The Duke's voice was that of a man who has to speak of something foul but has complete control over his disgust for it.

"I assure you, on my honour," The Kildonnon said, "that I had no knowledge of this."

"Then you were being deceived as I was!" the Duke answered. "Not only by your daughter, but by your sons, your nephews and doubtless your brother!"

Slowly The Kildonnon turned his head to look at his relatives, but they could not meet his eyes.

The Duke gave a short laugh that had no humour in it.

"Do you suppose that they were not aware that their cousin Neil was meeting my wife surreptitiously and clandestinely on every possible occasion?"

As there was no answer he went on:

"There were doubtless people of my Clan who could have told me where the Duchess went when she insisted on riding alone; who it was who waited for her on the Moors and in the woods; how letters were smuggled into the Castle, were carried over the border by those who were in the secret."

The Duke's tone was like a whip-lash. Now there was not only contempt in his voice but an anger that was irrepressible and which showed itself too in the fierce glint of his dark eyes.

"I do not know how long this degrading subterfuge would

have continued," he said, "if your daughter had not realised I was bound to learn of her perfidy because she was with child."

There was no doubt that this was a shock to The Kildonnon.

His hands clenched themselves as they rested on the arms of his chair and his brother's face seemed suddenly drained of colour.

"A child!" he repeated almost beneath his breath. "How did you learn of this?"

"Your daughter was obliging enough to leave me a letter telling me of the circumstances which had obliged her to leave for France with her paramour and cousin, Neil Kildonnon!"

Again the two sons of The Kildonnon glanced at each other and it was obvious they must have had some idea of where their sister was.

The Duke however was not looking at them. His eyes were still on their father's as he went on:

"As soon as I knew where the woman who bore my name and who carried another man's child had gone, I followed her."

"You went to France?" The Kildonnon's question was more of a growl.

"As I travelled by sea and they by land," the Duke replied, "I actually arrived in Calais ahead of them."

"What happened?"

It was Alister Kildonnon who asked the question as if he could not stand the suspense.

"I challenged Neil Kildonnon to a duel," the Duke answered, "and killed him!"

"Killed him!"

It was The Kildonnon who ejaculated the words and made them sound like an accusation.

"A perfectly honourable duel," the Duke said slowly, "where we were both attended by seconds and the referee was a man of repute."

"And he did not wound you?" Rory the elder of the Kildonnon sons asked the question.

The Duke, with a twist of his lips replied :

"Neil Kildonnon was never a particularly good shot!"

"But to – kill him!"

Alister Kildonnon also made his exclamation sound like an accusation.

"As a matter of fact," the Duke said coldly, "he took the best part of a day to die. He had medical attention and I believe everything possible was done to save his life."

"But he died!" The Kildonnon said. "And Margaret?"

"When she was told he was dead, your daughter stabbed herself in the heart with his skean-dhu."

"You could have prevented it! Surely you could have prevented it!" Rory Kildonnon shouted, jumping to his feet.

The Duke looked him up and down before he said :

"I had my wife taken to a Convent and placed in the care of the Nuns. Unfortunately, because she was in such pain, the doctor ordered her laudanum. The Nun who was nursing her gave her the prescribed dose and put the bottle down in another part of the bed-room."

The Duke looked away from the young man, who was still standing facing him aggressively, towards The Kildonnon.

"Somehow, and it must have been a superhuman effort," the Duke went on quietly, "Margaret struggled from her sick-bed and picking up the bottle, drank its entire contents."

The Kildonnon put his hand up to his eyes; it was the first gesture of weakness he had made up until now.

"She went into a coma," the Duke continued, "from which she never emerged."

"And that suited you, I suppose?" Rory Kildonnon asked angrily. "You were rid of both of them, Neil and my sister."

He went a step nearer to the Duke and there was something distinctly threatening about his out-thrust chin and clenched hands.

"You will sit down!" the Duke ordered sharply, "and listen to what else I have to tell you."

It seemed as if he would be defied but The Kildonnon took his hands from his eyes to say:

"Sit down, Rory. Margaret is dead and there is nothing we can do about it."

"And Neil is dead too!" Rory Kildonnon retorted, but he obeyed his Father.

The Duke looked at the men seated in front of him and then he said:

"There are two things you can do about this: you can either make sure that the true story of my wife's death is not known outside this room, or you can spread it abroad and our Clans will once again be at each others' throats."

He looked at Rory Kildonnon and the others as he spoke and he knew by the expression on their faces that to fight him at this moment would give them the utmost satisfaction.

But The Kildonnon spoke in a voice of authority.

"What you have told us, Arkcraig, will remain a secret. I have no desire for the memory of my daughter to be defamed. Nor do I wish to perpetuate a feud which has brought poverty and misery to the Kildonnons for too long."

"That certainly is the sensible course to take," the Duke replied. "But in view of the manner in which I have been treated, because of the humiliation I have endured, I have a condition to make to which you will agree."

The six Clansmen looked at him somewhat apprehensively. There was a change in his voice; and there was too something in his bearing which made them feel as if, without saying so in so many words, he issued a challenge.

"What is your condition?" The Kildonnon enquired.

"It is quite simple," the Duke replied. "I accepted a wife of your choosing. Now you will accept one of mine."

"A wife!" Alister Kildonnon exclaimed incredulously.

In answer the Duke took up a large silver bell which stood behind him on a table beside the Chieftain's chair.

He rang it and almost instantly the door into the room opened.

*　　*　　*

The road climbing the hillside wound between moors, brilliant with heather.

Every so often, when the horses disturbed them, a covey of grouse would rise and swing down the valley, flying, Tara thought, with a grace that was almost indescribable.

The whole way from where they had last spent the night she had been held spell-bound by the beauty of the country through which they were passing.

There were forests of deep dark pines which seemed full of mystery; bare mountains down which silver cascades fell glittering in the sunshine to disappear into the hidden depth of rocky crags.

The Lochs were even more beautiful than those she had already seen, and the sunshine turned them to gold so that she felt every mile they travelled this was a fairy land such as she never believed existed.

"Could anything be more lovely?" she asked and Mr. Falkirk, sitting beside her, laughed.

"You said that yesterday."

"And I shall say it tomorrow!" she answered. "If only we could go on driving for ever."

He knew she was worried about reaching the Castle and he thought himself that she had good reason for it.

He too was in some ways sorry that their journey must come to an end and he could not continue teaching this intelligent child.

"In a short time we shall see the Castle," he said as their horses topped a rise and started the down-hill descent into the next valley.

Tara turned from the window towards him.

"I am ... afraid," she said in a very low voice.

"I assure you it will not be as bad as you anticipate," he answered.

"It might be ... worse."

She gave a little sigh. Then there was an unmistakable lilt in her voice as she added:

"You will be ... there?"

"I shall be there," Mr. Falkirk said, "but you must understand, Tara, that I am the Comptroller to His Grace, and as such it would cause a great deal of comment or perhaps bad feeling were I to favour one servant above the others."

"I understand," Tara said, "but you promised I could borrow your books, and it will be possible to ... speak to you if things are ... unbearable."

"I promise you they will not be that," Mr. Falkirk replied sharply.

He had thought about Tara during the night and decided that he would impress upon the Duke her rather exceptional qualities and, unless His Grace had very decided opinions on the matter, try to get her put in the charge of the Housekeeper, a kindly woman who had been at the Castle for over thirty years.

"There is one thing I must not forget to give you," he said aloud, "and I have the feeling, Tara, it will give you courage."

He drew as he spoke from his waistcoat pocket the small gold locket which had belonged to her mother.

Tara gave a little cry of delight, and when he put it in her hands she looked down at it and he knew that he had given her something which did in fact bring her great happiness.

"Do you often think of your Mother?" he asked.

"I tell myself stories about her," Tara said, "and about my father."

He thought there was just a slight note of defiance in her voice as she said the last word, as if she almost dared him to point out that her father, whoever he might have been, had not condescended to marry her mother.

"I am glad you do that," Mr. Falkirk answered. "I have a feeling, Tara, that if you did not have such a vivid imagination your life, up to now, would have been much harder to bear."

"It was being able to read which made all the difference," Tara told him. "By reading I could escape from all the problems at the Orphanage. I could forget Mrs. Barrowfield, the lack of money and the fact that the children were always hungry."

"They will not be hungry any longer," Mr. Falkirk said, "you can be assured of that."

"I keep telling myself that all you have promised me is true," Tara replied, "and I think once the children are fed they will be far easier to handle."

"I am certain of that," Mr. Falkirk said reassuringly, "and, Tara, try to think about yourself for a change. You are starting a new life and I am very anxious it should be a happy one."

"It is ... frightening all the ... same," Tara murmured almost beneath her breath.

Then she smiled and it seemed to Mr. Falkirk that there was sunshine in her eyes.

"I tell you what I will do, Sir. I will put on my Mother's locket and every time I feel it lying against my skin I will know that it gives me courage. The kind of courage the Scots showed in their battles against the English."

"You have been reading about them," Mr. Falkirk smiled.

"Last night I was reading about Culloden," Tara replied. "Oh! Why could they have not won? It was such a muddle ... the Scottish troops wet and hungry; the English with the advantage of having cannon."

She looked away from him and out through the window.

She did not see the beauty of the moors, instead she saw the Clans, humbled, and defeated, the wounded and dying on the battlefield, the hated English triumphant, deliberately killing those who were still alive.

"The fighting is over," Mr. Falkirk said quietly. "What we have to work for now, Tara, is prosperity for the Scottish. Many are desperately poor and if they have any talents, apart from that of keeping themselves alive, they do not know how to use them."

"I wish I could help them," Tara said impulsively.

She gave a little laugh and added:

"How presumptuous that sounds, Sir, and I am only a Sassenach!"

"You cannot be sure of that," Mr. Falkirk said, "when you have a Scottish name."

"Is Tara Scottish?" she asked, "I always wondered."

"Of course it is Scottish," Mr. Falkirk said, "I should have thought the Minister would have told you that."

"We were usually talking about the Bible," Tara answered, "or the books that he lent me, and it never occurred to me to ask him about myself."

Her eyes were shining as she went on :

"But you have told me something very wonderful. Now that I know I have a Scottish name, I shall dream that I belong to this beautiful country; and just as the Scots are brave, I will be brave too."

Mr. Falkirk thought there was something very moving in the way she spoke, but before he could say any more the Coach came to a sudden standstill.

"I wonder what is happening?" he exclaimed and put his head out of the open window.

To his surprise he saw it was a groom riding a horse and wearing the Duke's Livery who had brought the Coach to a standstill.

The man dismounted and holding his horse by the bridle, came towards him.

"Good-day to ye, Mr. Falkirk."

"Good day, Andrew."

"I've a message for ye, Sir, from His Grace."

"What is it?" Mr. Falkirk enquired.

"His Grace asks, Sir, that ye should arrive at the Castle at precisely ten minutes to five. Ye will proceed to the landing outside the Chieftain's Room and wait there until His Grace bids ye enter by the ringing of a bell."

Mr. Falkirk looked surprised.

"I am not to get in touch with His Grace beforehand?"

"No, Sir, but when His Grace rings ye and the person ye've brought with ye are to go into the Chieftain's Room."

The groom spoke as if he had learnt the message off by heart, parrot-wise.

When he had finished speaking, Mr. Falkirk said :

"Is that all?"

"Yes, Sir."

"Thank you, Andrew."

The groom saluted, remounted his horse and with a grin

at the footmen, he set off ahead of them down the road up which he had come.

Mr. Falkirk drew his watch from his pocket and spoke to the footman who had descended and was standing by the carriage, obviously awaiting his instructions.

"If we go straight to the Castle now, we shall be too early. We will stop at the Inn at the top of the next Glen."

"Very good, Sir."

The horses started off again and as Mr. Falkirk sat back Tara said nervously:

"Why should His Grace wish me to accompany you to the Chieftain's Room?"

"I have not the slightest idea," Mr. Falkirk said with a note of irritation in his voice.

He found the Duke's instructions incomprehensible and it made him angry.

Surely all this mystery was quite unnecessary, just as it had been unnecessary in the first place to bring a girl from the Orphanage to Scotland.

But because he knew it would perturb Tara he controlled his feelings and deliberately started to talk of other things for the next two miles they must travel before they came to the Inn.

It was a poor place but the tea that was put in front of them on Mr. Falkirk's order was in Tara's eyes a sumptuous meal.

There were baps and girdle cakes, hot and fresh from the fire, and there was home-made butter to spread on oat-cakes which she had never tasted before.

"Are all teas in Scotland like this?" she asked.

"A Scottish housewife prides herself on her baking," Mr. Falkirk answered, "and I commend the Scottish teas to you, Tara, because although you are not as thin as you were when we started out on this journey, there is still room for improvement."

She smiled at him a little shyly and he saw there were no longer deep hollows in her cheeks and the lines under her eyes had faded.

She was still, however, very slim and he wondered how

she would fare in the cold winter nights when the icy winds would whistle down from the snows on the mountains to wail round the Castle, and even the huge open fires which burnt in every room could not keep out the cold.

'She will need warmer clothing than she is wearing at the moment,' and he decided that was another thing he must bring to the notice of the Duke.

Then he told himself with a laugh at his own expense that he was behaving like an anxious hen over one small chick.

The Duke would think him insane if he started discussing with him the inadequacies of a servant's clothing.

As Comptroller he had full powers to do what he thought good in the household, but he knew were he to single Tara out for preferential treatment it would be fiercely resented by the rest of the staff.

"What is troubling you, Sir?" Tara asked.

It did not surprise Mr. Falkirk that she was so perceptive where he was concerned. He had learnt as soon as they began this journey that she was as sensitive to his moods and feelings as she was to his thoughts.

"I suppose you would feel flattered if I said I was worrying about you?"

"I should be very, very . . . honoured," she said in a low voice. "You have been so kind to me. I had no idea anyone could be so kind, and I think that is why I am frightened of losing you and being on my own."

"I shall be in the Castle," Mr. Falkirk said.

But he knew it was an inadequate statement and not what she wanted to hear.

She was silent a moment and then she said:

"Is His Grace very . . . frightening?"

She paused a moment, then added:

"I know, of course, I shall not normally be in contact with him, but he has sent for me and I shall see him when I arrive."

"I think this is again when you have to remember your Scottish blood," Mr. Falkirk said, "and tell yourself you are afraid of nothing and nobody."

He noticed as he spoke that Tara almost instinctively put up her hand to touch the locket where it lay beneath her dress between her breasts.

"I shall think of that," she said, "and pretend that my Clan, whichever it may be, is just as important as the Mc-Craigs."

"I am sure that was the truth," Mr. Falkirk replied.

He was rewarded by a sparkle in Tara's eyes and a smile which seemed to transform her whole face.

Nevertheless when they set off again the smile had gone, and she was looking serious and clearly nervous as the horses carried them down the valley, in through the great wrought-iron gates and up the drive towards the Castle.

When she first saw it standing high on the hillside, its towers and battlements silhouetted against the sky, Mr. Falkirk heard her draw in her breath.

He had seen it so often, but even so its beauty and its majesty always struck him afresh every time he returned home.

It was awe-inspiring and at the same time there was something steadfast and stalwart about it which made him, although he was not a McCraig, know why to the Clansmen it was a symbol of protection and of confidence.

It was almost as if so long as the Castle stood they would exist.

He thought what those who were evicting the Highlanders and had scattered their Clans had given the Scots, was a feeling of despair, of living in a world in which they could be sure of nothing, not even hope.

But Arkcraig Castle personified everything which made a Scotsman feel pride in himself and in the blood that flowed through his veins.

Its very strength and stability told them that not for nothing had men died for the causes in which they believed, and the glory that came from dedication to an ideal.

The horses were pulling up the last incline of the drive.

The coachman was urging them to arrive with a flourish, conscious as he did so that his achievement in driving all the way from London to the Castle was something that the younger men would envy.

"It is very ... large."

It was the first time Tara had spoken for over ten minutes.

Mr. Falkirk smiled at her as the Coach drew to a standstill at the front door.

"You will get used to it," he said, "and remember however big it is your home, as it is mine."

She smiled back at him a little tremulously. Then the coach door opened and the servants were welcoming Mr. Falkirk back.

They took Tara's black cloak from her shoulders and she and Mr. Falkirk walked slowly up the wide stone staircase to the landing.

She had a quick glance at the stags' heads which decorated the huge Hall, at the shields and Claymores which made a pattern over the fire-place; at the flags, some of them tattered, hanging from the banisters.

Then she was only conscious that her heart was thumping in her breast and her mouth felt dry.

The servants in their kilts seemed to her almost like soldiers, and she thought the Major Domo who had preceded them was so impressive that she would not have been surprised to be told that he was the Duke himself.

She had taken the opportunity when they were having tea at the Inn to change into a clean uncreased dress.

Mr. Falkirk had not suggested that she should do this, and expecting she would be able to change as soon as she arrived at the Castle, she had therefore placed it on the top of her baggage.

It had not taken her long at the Inn, and as she washed the dust from her face she thought, as Mr. Falkirk had, that she did not look as thin and emaciated as when she had left the Orphanage.

She also felt better than she had ever felt in her life. The exhaustion that had sometimes made her feel that she was sinking into the ground, and which she was sensible enough to know was due to lack of food, had gone.

Each morning as she awoke on the journey she felt more energetic than she had the day before, and every night when she went to bed she was not too tired to read at least a chapter from the books Mr. Falkirk had lent her.

At the back of her mind there was the fear that if she was not strong enough for the work the Duke required of her, she might be sent back to London or, more terrible still, to another Orphanage in Scotland.

It would be humiliating to find she was not competent to undertake her duties.

What was worse, as she was a nameless orphan, she could not be dismissed as another servant could be, to go home and try to find other employment.

So she would have to be found a place somewhere else and her only reference would be from the Orphanage which belonged to the Duke.

"I must not fail! I must not!" Tara said to herself as she looked into the mirror at the Inn, and because she was worried she had adjusted the grey cotton cap on her head.

The sides of it covered her ears which she had always thought was a mistake, because some of the children were hard of hearing and it made it more difficult for them.

As far as she was concerned she could hear perfectly even with her ears covered.

But she had thought the cap very ugly and hoped once again that the Duke would allow her to dress in ordinary clothes so that she would not appear so conspicuous.

She felt now as she and Mr. Falkirk reached the landing that the Scottish servants must be staring at her and that her grey cotton dress was very drab beside the bright colours of their tartan and the polished buttons on their jackets.

"You have His Grace's instructions, Sir?" she heard the Major Domo ask.

Mr. Falkirk nodded.

Now he was in the Castle Tara thought he seemed to have assumed a different bearing. There was something definitely authoritative about him; something which made her realise that he was, as the Duke's Comptroller, an important person.

Behind a huge oak door they could hear the murmur of voices but it was impossible to distinguish what was being said.

As Mr. Falkirk did not speak, Tara stood beside him in silence, feeling every moment the tension in her body mounting almost like a wave, creeping up her breast and into her very throat.

Then suddenly so loud it made her jump there was the sound of a bell.

The Major Domo glanced at Mr. Falkirk and his hand went out towards the handle of the door. He opened it and in a stentorian tone announced:

"Mr. Falkirk, Your Grace!"

As the Comptroller walked ahead of her, Tara had the impression that the huge room was as brilliant as a rainbow with tartan. Then her eyes went towards one man standing ahead and she knew it was the Duke.

He was just as she had expected him to look, only even more frightening.

He seemed to stand out and tower over not only the men sitting in front of him but over the room itself.

Never had she imagined a man could look so distinguished, so important and so magnificent.

From what Mr. Falkirk had said she had expected him to be good-looking, but not so handsome with clear-cut features, or at the same time looking so disdainful and contemptuous.

She thought he was angry and she felt an unmistakable atmosphere of tension that was almost explosive.

She thought it must have come from the other gentlemen sitting in the chairs who had all turned their eyes towards her and were staring in an unaccountable manner which made her feel both shy and frightened.

The fear that had risen in her made her, for a moment, so panic-stricken that she felt as if her legs would no longer support her.

But then, almost as if it spoke to her, she felt her Mother's locket between her breasts and told herself that she was a Scot and these Scotsmen could not drive her away.

Her chin went up a little and as she stood a little behind Mr. Falkirk she heard him say:

"Good afternoon, Your Grace."

"Good afternoon, Falkirk. I must congratulate you on being on time."

The Duke's voice was deep, Tara thought, and it had a resonance about it which made it different to any man's voice she had heard before.

Although she was shy she was unable to prevent herself from looking at him, and as she did so she thought that when he was in the room it would be difficult to remember that anyone else was there.

She was aware that his eyes were on Mr. Falkirk and he had not seemed even to glance in her direction. Now as the door shut behind them he said slowly and distinctly :

"I have informed The Kildonnon, Falkirk, of the events which took place in France, and he and his relatives have agreed that outside these four walls no one shall ever be aware of what occurred there."

Mr. Falkirk bowed his head.

"Just before you arrived," the Duke went on, "I informed The Kildonnon that after our agreement a year ago, I permitted him to choose my wife for me because we considered it to be in the interests of our Clans. I now claim for myself the privilege of choice."

He looked at Tara.

"On my instructions," he went on, "you have brought my future wife with you."

Mr. Falkirk stiffened and Tara stared at the Duke in bewilderment. She had not understood what he was saying.

The Duke turned to The Kildonnon.

"I have chosen," he said, "a girl who is unpolluted by the world or by her relatives because she has none. She comes from 'The Orphanage of the Nameless' and I think you will agree that to fulfil the functions that you required of the Duchess of Arkcraig there could in the present circumstances be no-one more eminently suitable than – a bastard!"

For a moment there was only silence. Then Rory Kildonnon and his brother jumped to their feet.

"You insult us, Arkcraig, and we will not stand for it!"

They advanced threateningly towards the Duke as they

spoke, but a faint smile twisted his lips as he replied:

"The alternative remains open, gentlemen: you can return the ten thousand pounds that I lent your Father and you can declare war on me and on my Clan. But let me inform you once and for all that what land we take from you in the ensuing battle we shall hold!"

"You cannot do this!" Rory Kildonnon shouted hotly. "We will go to Edinburgh, we will sue you in the Courts."

"And what compensation will they give you for your burnt crops, for your lost cattle, for your dead sheep?" the Duke asked scornfully. "Will they send soldiers to protect you? Can you afford a long drawn-out legal battle?"

The two young men stood indecisive, and now The Kildonnon rose and with a gesture of his hand waved them back from the menacing position they had taken up.

"Your terms are harsh, Arkcraig," he said quietly.

"But at least they are honest," the Duke answered. "I am not cheating you as you cheated me."

The eyes of the two Chieftains met and it seemed for a moment there was a battle of wills between them. Then The Kildonnon capitulated:

"You know as well as I do that we have no alternative but to do anything you ask of us."

"But if . . ." Rory Kildonnon expostulated.

The Kildonnon turned on him.

"This is my decision, and you will all do as I say."

"Very well," the Duke said, "and because I intend that you shall accept the position without reserve, you will now be present at my marriage and you will then pay homage, each one of you, to the new Duchess of Arkcraig."

Once again the young Kildonnons would have burst out in protest if their Father had not glowered at them and then nodded to the Duke.

"We agree, Arkcraig."

As he was determined to extort an acceptance from each one of them, the Duke looked at The Kildonnon's brother, Alister, to ask:

"Do you agree?"

There was a little pause and the elder man swallowed before he replied in a voice that was hardly audible:

"I agree."

"And you, Rory Kildonnon?" the Duke enquired.

The young man looked at his Father as if to appeal against the intolerable situation that was being forced upon them. But The Kildonnon was frowning and after a moment he could only say surlily:

"I agree."

The same reply was extorted from his brother and his twin cousins. Then the Duke turned to Mr. Falkirk.

"Will you ask the Minister to come in. You will find him waiting in the Study."

Mr. Falkirk bowed, not daring to trust his voice. He turned and went from the room leaving Tara standing forlornly by herself.

She was too frightened, too utterly bewildered to move.

She only knew that something so incredible, so extraordinary was happening that she felt as if her brain had ceased to function and the Duke was speaking a foreign language she did not understand.

Then as the Kildonnons murmured amongst themselves the Duke walked towards her, and with an effort, because she felt she was in a night-mare from which she could not awake, she dropped him a curtsy.

"What is your name?"

His voice was very low and deep.

"T . Tara ... Y . your ... Grace."

She stammered over the simple words.

"You heard what I said, Tara, you are to marry me. How old are you?"

"Nearly eighteen, Your Grace."

The Duke raised his eyebrows.

"Older than I expected. You have lived in the Orphanage all your life?"

"Y . yes, Your Grace."

"You have not become involved in any love affair?"

"No ... of course not ... Your Grace."

"You are sure of that?"

"V . very sure ... Your G . Grace."

The door opened and the Minister came into the Chieftain's Room followed by Mr. Falkirk. He was wearing his black Cassock with the white muslin tabs at his throat and carried a prayer-book in his hand.

He bowed to the Duke and then to the Kildonnons.

"You have come here, Minister," the Duke said, "to join me in matrimony with Tara, who has no other name. These gentlemen, whom I think you know, will be witnesses to the ceremony."

"Very good, Your Grace."

The Minister spoke with a broad Scottish accent. Then he moved to the far end of the room and stood in front of the fire-place that was surmounted with the huge emblem of the McCraigs carved in stone.

He waited with a dignity that was impressive, turning the pages of his Prayer-book as he did so.

The Duke offered his arm to Tara and for a moment she did not understand what he intended.

Then shyly, feeling as if she had no will, no mind of her own, she placed her fingers on the inside of his arm and he led her forward until they stood in front of the Minister.

Mr. Falkirk remained just inside the door. The Minister began the Service.

It was very short and although Tara had never been to a wedding, she had read the Marriage Service in her Prayer-book and realised that the English version was very different.

Yet there was no mistaking what was happening when the Minister said:

"Heron Torquil, 5th Duke of Arkcraig, Chieftain of the Clan McCraig, will you be joined in Holy Matrimony, according to the Will of God, to this woman, Tara?"

"I will!"

The words were spoken firmly and defiantly.

"Tara, will you take this man to be your husband, to obey him, to be in subjection under him and to serve him for the rest of your life until death do you part?"

"I will."

Tara's voice was hardly above a whisper. The Minister

joined their hands and the Duke put a ring upon her finger which was far too big.

A prayer was said over them which Tara was incapable of hearing or understanding.

She was married! Married to a man she had never seen until two minutes before!

A man, whom the very thought of seeing had frightened her all the way to Scotand!

A man, whom she had now seen, and was even more frightening than she had anticipated.

She was married!

Chapter Four

"Shall I help you undress – Your Grace?"

There was a perceptible pause before the last two words.

"N . no .. no, thank you," Tara answered nervously.

"As this room has not been used for some time I lit a fire. It can be chilly in the evenings, even though it is summer."

"Thank you, Mrs. McCraig. It is ... very ... kind of you."

The Housekeeper looked round the room.

"There is nothing else I can do for you ... Your Grace?"

Again there was a pause before the last words.

"No thank you."

The Housekeeper went from the room and Tara was alone. She stood in the huge high-ceilinged bed-room where she had learnt the wife of the Chieftain had slept since the Castle was first built.

Originally she supposed it must have been plain and bare, but now it was furnished with a luxury and an elegance which she found frightening.

The huge canopied bed with its embroidered curtains was the type of sleeping place she had never envisaged herself occupying, even in her dreams!

The elegant inlaid furniture; the mirrors with their gilt frames; the pictures on the walls, all seemed over-powering to someone as inconsequential as herself.

And yet she was the Duchess of Arkcraig!

Tara could understand only too well why it was difficult for the Housekeeper to address her as such and it would be the same, she thought, for everyone else in the Castle.

Slowly she began to undress and as she took off her grey cotton dress she shuddered.

She had been ashamed of her appearance when after the

marriage service, Mrs. McCraig, the Housekeeper, had showed her the way to her room.

They had passed along passages hung with pictures of the Arkcraig ancestors and Tara felt they must all be looking at her contemptuously.

It had been uncomfortable too to find two maids lifting the few garments she possessed from the wicker-basket in which she had brought them to Scotland.

She had known that the servants were as astonished by her meagre possessions as they were by her new position.

Not that she could realise it herself. She still felt numb as if her brain had ceased to function; it was impossible to comprehend what had happened, or to contemplate what lay ahead.

She longed to find Mr. Falkirk to ask for his reassurance and guidance. But when the Kildonnons had been forced to pay her homage and had done so in a sullen, resentful silence before they left the Castle, Mr. Falkirk had not been in the room.

He had reappeared when the last of the Kildonnons had disappeared down the broad staircase, leaving behind them an atmosphere which Tara knew was one of hatred.

She had turned to him with an expression of relief in her eyes, but before he could speak the Duke said:

"I want to talk to you, Falkirk. I suggest we go into my Study."

"Very good, Your Grace."

It was then Mrs. McCraig had appeared and Tara thought she had been ordered to do so by Mr. Falkirk.

"This, Mrs. McCraig, is the new Duchess of Arkcraig," the Duke had said in a cold voice. "Will you show Her Grace to her apartments and see to her comfort."

Mrs. McCraig had curtsied, and as she was led away, Tara thought despairingly that she was walking into a new life and had not the least idea of what she should do about it.

She learnt however that the Duke dined early, that she was expected to take a bath before dinner and to change her dress.

She had only one other clean gown with her and it was more threadbare than the other two.

The clothes at the Orphanage were passed from orphan to orphan until they fell into rags and could only be used for cleaning the floors.

Those leaving to become apprentices did not take their charity garments with them. They were left behind for another orphan of the same size.

As Tara had been so long in the Orphanage, her clothes had in fact been new because she made them herself.

She was quite certain that Mrs. Barrowfield would not have provided her with the money to buy material but the previous Duchess of Arkcraig had frugally purchased at a reduced price roll upon roll of the grey cotton.

It was therefore only a question of finding time to make herself a new dress. But this was perhaps the most difficult task of all as Tara had very little time to herself with so many children to look after.

She remembered now it was over two years since she had had a new gown and wished that she had been able to make just one before she was taken North. Then she told herself that now she was the Duke's wife, she would be able to wear something different.

"The Duke's wife!"

She repeated the words to herself as she washed in the bath that had been carried into the bed-room and set down on a large Turkish rug on which she could dry her feet.

It was a luxury she had seldom experienced, to have a hot bath all to herself and know that she need not hurry over it.

The water was very soft and slightly brown in colour and Tara looked at it in surprise until she realised it was the peaty water Mr. Falkirk had told her she would find in Scotland.

The two maids had brought the bath into the room. Although they had greeted Tara politely, she realised they were shy and because she felt she had nothing to say to them they waited on her in silence.

When she was dressed and wondering what she should do, Mrs. McCraig returned.

Tara realised that the elderly woman was regarding her coldly and there was a stiffness in her manner which she could understand.

The Housekeeper obviously resented a charity child becoming her mistress and who could blame her?

But because there was no-one else whom she could ask, Tara said nervously:

"Will ... you tell me ... what I do ... now?"

There was something childlike in her anxiety and Mrs. McCraig's hard features relaxed.

"You're nervous, Your Grace, and it's not surprising," she replied. "The Castle is awful big when you first see it."

"It is!" Tara agreed.

"I gathered from Mr. Falkirk that you were not expecting to find yourself the wife of His Grace."

"No indeed!" Tara replied, "so please tell me what I should do."

"There'll be dinner in a few minutes," Mrs. McCraig said, "and you'll be dining with His Grace. You'll meet him in the Chieftain's Room, the room where you were married."

"I think I know where it is," Tara murmured.

"Then go along there. You'll find His Grace waiting for you."

Tara stifled a longing to ask Mrs. McCraig to come with her.

Instead forlornly, feeling as if she were little more than a grey ghost, she moved along the wide passage which led to the Chieftain's Room.

Only as she nearly reached it did she hear voices and recognised Mr. Falkirk's.

Since he was there, things would not be so bad, she thought. Then as she approached nearer she heard him say:

"I was thinking, Your Grace, that you will wish to send a carriage to Edinburgh tomorrow as soon as it is light."

"To Edinburgh?" the Duke enquired. "Why should I wish to do that?"

"I imagine you would wish to purchase clothes for the new Duchess. There is no place nearer, as Your Grace is well aware, that would have gowns in any way appropriate either in material or style."

There was a silence for a moment and then Tara heard the Duke say:

"The Duchess is appropriately dressed and I see no reason to change her attire."

"Your Grace . . ." Mr. Falkirk began to expostulate.

"I intend," the Duke interrupted, "that she shall be a symbol to the Kildonnons of everything that they themselves omitted to provide in the person of the previous Duchess."

He paused for a moment and then he said:

"As she moves among the women, The Kildonnon will see her and find it impossible to forget the manner in which his daughter behaved and the shame she has inflicted upon me."

As she was listening to what was being said Tara had still walked forward almost automatically, without thinking what she was doing.

Now as Mr. Falkirk was about to argue with his employer, he saw her standing in the door-way of the Chieftain's Room.

Her cheeks were very pale, her eyes almost too large for her small face had a stricken expression in them, and he checked the words he was about to speak.

Instead he bowed to the Duke and walked from the room.

Only as he passed Tara did he look at her and she knew that he was angry at the Duke's decision but there was nothing he could do about it.

"I hope you have been well looked after."

The Duke's voice was sharp and because Tara felt nervous it took her a few seconds to answer him.

"Y . yes . . . thank you . . . Your Grace."

"You must be tired after such a long journey, but tomorrow you will be able to explore the Castle and the grounds. I am sure you will find them interesting."

"Yes . . . Your Grace."

She felt as if he was speaking to her as if she were a casual acquaintance of no particular interest and his thoughts were elsewhere. As the Butler announced dinner, he looked round with what she thought was an expression of relief on his face.

He had changed, she noticed, from the clothes he had been wearing when she had first seen him speaking to the Kildonnons.

Now his jacket was of black velvet, ornamented with silver buttons and there was a jabot of priceless lace at his throat.

Tara thought, although she was not certain, that his Sporran was much more elaborate than the one he had worn previously.

Never had she imagined that any man could look so magnificent, and yet at the same time his clothes seemed entirely right and not in the least theatrical.

As dinner was announced he offered her his arm as he had done before and now she knew what she was expected to do.

He led her across the wide landing with its stone balustrade and into a room on the other side of it which she realised was the Dining Hall.

This too was very large with high ceilings and long narrow windows, looking, she was to find later, onto the front of the Castle.

For a moment she felt almost blinded by the polished cups of gold and silver which decorated the long table beside the enormous candelabra each containing six lighted candles.

There was a high-backed chair for the Duke at the top of the table; Tara sat on his right and looked in bewilderment at the long array of knives, forks and spoons – even Mr. Falkirk's teaching had not prepared her for so many.

As if the Duke had nothing to say to her he talked to the Butler as they were being served.

"Was this salmon caught today?"

"Yes, Your Grace."

"Who brought it in?"

"Ross, Your Grace."

"Did he gaff or net it?"

"I understand it was gaffed, Your Grace."

"I have told him before not to use gaff on too small a fish!"

"I will remind him, Your Grace."

"I will speak to him to-morrow. Tell Mr. Falkirk I wish to see him in the morning!"

"Yes, Your Grace."

Dinner seemed to stretch out endlessly, as course succeeded course.

Tara noticed the Duke's eyes were dark and glowering and he ate very little. Because she was so frightened she found it almost impossible to swallow.

Mr. Falkirk had persuaded her on the last part of their journey to eat what had seemed to her an excessive amount at every meal; but now, though she felt ashamed when she thought how precious this food was, she could not finish even the tiny amount she had on her plate.

She was offered wine but refused it, and when dessert was put on the table, huge peaches, such as she had never seen before, and black grapes with velvet bloom on them, she thought with relief that the meal must be nearly at the end.

Suddenly, somewhere in the distance, she heard the shrill high note of music and when it came nearer and still nearer she knew that she was hearing for the first time the Pipes.

She held her breath as swinging into the room there came a Clansman in the McCraig tartan, his bonnet on the side of his head.

His plaid hung from his shoulder and his kilt swung from his hips as he marched round the table making sounds that seemed to Tara she must have heard in her dreams.

He played two tunes, before he came to attention beside the Duke's chair to ask:

"Have ye any choice this eve', Ye Grace?"

He spoke with such a Scottish accent that it was hard to understand what he said and the Duke gave him an order in a language which Tara knew was Gaelic.

Then once more the Piper was encircling the table and the music seemed to sweep out to fill the room and to be part of the moors and the beautiful wild country outside.

Finally he finished and once again he stood waiting.

The Butler placed by the Duke's side a small silver cup which the Duke handed to the Piper.

The Piper raised it in the gesture of a toast:

"*Shlainte*," he said and drained the cup in one draught.

He saluted, walked from the room and for the first time it seemed since they had eaten together the Duke looked at Tara.

"I hope you enjoyed hearing the Pipes?"

"It was wonderful," she answered. "I always imagined somehow they would be like that."

"Like what?"

"That they would make you want to laugh and cry simultaneously, and make you hear the voices of the Scots speaking from their hearts."

The Duke looked at her in surprise.

"Do they really make you feel like that?"

"I wish I could express myself better," Tara answered. "Mr. Falkirk told me how important the Piper is to a Clan. Now I understand how men can be rallied to fight for their faith and not be afraid to die."

Her voice was very soft. She was thinking of Culloden and remembering how the story of the Scots defeat at the hands of the English had distressed her.

"How can you talk – or rather think like that?"

The Duke's question made her feel shy, and she lapsed into silence. Perhaps he thought her over-emotional or worse still, presumptuous in speaking in such a manner.

Now, as she undressed in the big bed-room, Tara found herself remembering how stirred to her very soul she had felt by the music.

'It made me certain that I am a Scot,' she thought whimsically.

She wished she could live in Scotland in a small croft and get to know the people who lived in such places and understand their problems; their difficulties and perhaps too their despair.

"I have always wanted to help," she told herself, "and as the Duchess of Arkcraig, I may be able to do so."

She still could not realise that she was not only the Duchess but a married woman. She looked down at the ring on her finger. It was too big and she was afraid of losing it.

Suddenly a thought struck her!

She was the Duke's wife, and a wife was part of her husband. They were made one by the marriage service.

She had been so bemused and bewildered since she arrived at the Castle that it was only now that the full implication of what her marriage might mean seemed to hit her as if it were a blow.

"The Duke is my husband!"

She repeated the words almost under her breath and then she began to tremble and though instinctively she drew nearer to the fire, she could feel no warmth from it.

'I am afraid,' she thought and wanted to run away, or find Mr. Falkirk and ask him what she should do.

Although in the Orphanage there was continual talk of the orphans being illegitimate, and of their mothers having sinned against God and against the Church, Tara had never wondered what such a sin actually implied.

An unmarried woman gave birth to a baby who through no fault of its own was stigmatised, sneered at, and must in some way make reparation for not bearing its father's name.

But she had not the slightest idea what actually brought the child into being in the first place. Yet now it might, whatever it was, happen to her.

Because it was something which caused so much fuss and commotion it seemed menacing and she was terrified of the unknown.

"What shall I do? What can I do?" she asked aloud.

She felt as if the huge room with all its luxury was a trap into which she had stepped unwittingly and from which there was no escape.

She stared at the canopied bed with its frilled pillowcases; its velvet cover on which was embroidered the Duke's monogram surmounted by a coronet.

She shuddered. There was something terrifying in the

turned-back linen sheets, almost as if they invited her to participate in something that was too horrifying to contemplate.

There was a thick white lambskin rug spread in front of the fire and because she felt cold and at the same time weak, Tara sat down on it.

She held out her hands to the flames but they still could not warm her and her eyes were on the door – not the door which opened onto the passage – but another which she suspected led into the Duke's bed-room.

He was the Chieftain of the McCraigs, and he would come to her because he was her husband!

* * *

The Duke, having sent Tara to bed after their dinner was finished, went into the Chieftain's Room to pull back the curtains from one of the windows and to stand at the open casement looking down at the garden below.

Beyond lay the great loch and now the last glimmer of the sun was setting red and golden behind the moors and the first stars were coming out in the sky.

There was a serenity and beauty about it which did nothing to assuage the feeling of anger that possessed the Duke.

It had been a tumultuous tempest within his breast ever since he had sailed to France in pursuit of his wife and Neil Kildonnon.

He had not been in love when he married, but Margaret with her dark eyes and black hair had been extremely attractive.

He had thought that, since their marriage was based on good common sense and the betterment of their Clans, they would live amicably and she would fulfil the duties of a Duchess in the way his mother had done.

When The Kildonnon had suggested that the best way to get their Clansmen to accept that the days of feuding and warring were over was for him to marry a Kildonnon, he had instinctively wished to refuse.

Then he told himself it was just prejudice and that the centuries-old belief that every member of the Kildonnon

Clan was their natural enemy was so ridiculous and so out of date that it was up to him to set an example.

The marriage had taken place very quickly after it was first suggested for the simple reason that it was otherwise almost impossible to stop the incessant warring of their Clansmen.

There were many more McCraigs than there were Kildonnons, and the weaker Clan was becoming more impoverished every month that passed.

The Duke was honest enough to admit that he had in fact felt it was a condescension on his part to take Margaret Kildonnon as his wife, and be prepared at the same time to finance her relatives.

It had been a shock to his self-esteem and his pride that on the night of the marriage she had driven him from her bed-room with bitter words.

She told him that she would rather die than submit to the indignity of his embraces, and that while she would do her duty publicly, in private the feud their ancestors had carried on for centuries would still exist between them.

"I hate you," Margaret had said, her black eyes blazing. "I hate you and I hate every McCraig! Only if you all lay dead at my feet would I rejoice that the world was rid of its vermin."

There was something almost insane in the way that she spoke. Yet because he felt he could not live a life-time of such bitterness within his home, the Duke had hoped that time would change her.

He was sorry for her in that she had spent twenty-three years of her life in the dilapidated, uncomfortable, half-ruined Castle that The Kildonnon could not afford to modernise.

There had been no question for Margaret of going to Edinburgh for the Balls, Assemblies, Theatres, that every other girl of her age enjoyed.

There was not any money for travelling even from one part of Scotland to another and certainly none for pretty gowns or good horses.

"I can give her all these things," the Duke had said to himself and thought she would come to appreciate them.

He had been mistaken and he still felt the shock that was almost like a dagger-thrust when he had learnt from his wife's letter that because she was having a child by another man she had been forced to leave Scotland.

"You will never see me again," she wrote. "I am not asking your forgiveness for I need nothing from you except that you should leave us in peace."

That was something the Duke had not been prepared to do. Whatever she was like, however much she hated him, Margaret was his wife and the man who had seduced her away should pay the penalty.

As it happened, even though his blood had cried for revenge and a hatred of his Kildonnon ancestors had fanned the flame of his fury, he had not meant to kill Neil.

He had intended to maim or perhaps cripple him so at least he would not prove a very satisfactory lover. But Neil had died of his wounds and Margaret, fanatic to the end, had killed herself.

It was almost as if by dying they had cheated the Duke of his revenge and he had known when he had summoned the Kildonnons to the Castle, that he had wanted them to suffer as he suffered.

Just as Margaret had struck at his pride, he had struck at theirs.

It had been a satisfaction to know how much they were loathing him while he forced them to be present at his marriage and pay homage to his new Duchess – a bastard from an Orphanage, a girl born in sin, who would take the place of The Kildonnon's daughter.

As if his thoughts had brought him to Tara the Duke told himself that she would be waiting for him upstairs.

This time he would tolerate no scenes or refusal on his wedding night! He would make sure of an heir to the Dukedom and more important, to the leadership of the Clan.

Resolutely he turned from the window and walked to his bed-room.

85

His valet was waiting for him and without speaking he assisted the Duke to take off his magnificent attire.

Only as the man drew the skean-dhu from his left leg did the Duke think of Margaret and wonder if she would have killed herself or perhaps used such a weapon on him if he had insisted on his rights the first night they were married?

The skean-dhu had been adopted by the Scots after the dirks were forbidden by the English.

For thirty-five years the Dress Act had made it illegal for any man or boy to wear the plaid, the kilt, the shoulder belt, or any part of the Highland clothes.

Even the Pipes had been banned as the Duke of Cumberland said he had first-class evidence they were "instruments of war".

However the short knife called the skean-dhu was small enough to be concealed in the pocket or stuffed in the top of a stocking and when the Highlanders returned to their tartan, the skean-dhu remained a part of their dress.

No-one would ever know, the Duke thought to himself, except Mr. Falkirk, himself and the Kildonnons, that Margaret had stabbed herself with the sharp pointed knife.

But because she was a woman who bore his name, it would be impossible not to remember her every time he handled his skean-dhu.

The thought of her made him angry and there was a dark look on his face so that his valet looked at him apprehensively when he said:

"Good-night, Your Grace."

"Good-night!"

The Duke's voice made the simple words sound as if they were a malediction rather than an expression of goodwill.

Hastily the valet shut the door behind him and wiped his forehead before he walked away down the corridor.

The Duke stood for a moment in the centre of his room; the room in which his forefathers had slept and died; a room in which they had planned their battles against the English and their forays against the Kildonnons; a room which had known not only hate but love and happiness.

It was almost, the Duke thought, as if those who had

gone before him were telling him that whatever his difficulties the line must go on; the Clan must continue and there must be a Chieftain to rule it.

He squared his chin and then still with the darkness in his eyes, his mouth set in a hard line, he opened the communicating door between his room and the one traditionally occupied by the Chieftain's wife.

The first thing he noticed was that the room was in shadow and the candles were unlit.

He thought that perhaps he had been longer than he had imagined while thinking back into the past, and that after so many days of travelling Tara was tired and therefore had fallen asleep while waiting for him.

He walked to the bed, but when he reached it he saw with astonishment, in the faint light which came from the fire, that it was empty and unslept in.

Then he turned and saw Tara lying asleep on the rug in front of the fire-place.

He walked across the room to stand looking down at her and saw that while her long eyelashes were dark against her white skin, her hair which was no longer covered by her cap was a dark flaming red.

It was very short, growing not more than two inches from her head, but it curled riotously in a manner which picked up the light from the flames and made it seem as if she was haloed in burnished gold.

She had turned a little sideways, her face towards the fire as if she sought the warmth of it, and one hand had fallen open beside her, palm upwards.

She was wearing, the Duke noticed, a coarse calico night-gown that he expected was part of the orphan's uniform. It fastened high at the neck and close at the wrists and must have been harsh against a soft skin.

He could see her small feet peeping beneath it and there was something very vulnerable in the way in which she was lying and in the expression on her face.

He had the idea that she had been afraid before she fell asleep as there was a wistful droop at the corners of her mouth.

The Duke stood looking down at her and then because she was so young and so helpless the anger and the resolution went from his eyes.

He turned to the bed and pulled off the velvet cover. He folded it and gently laid it over her.

She did not stir.

The light from the flames danced on her curls and made them seem as if they were alive.

With a faint cynical twist to his lips, the Duke went from the room, closing the communicating door behind him.

* * *

Tara walked into the Chieftain's Room to find the Duke standing at the window, a letter in his hand.

She stood looking at him closely, not wishing to interrupt his concentration, at the same time knowing she must ask his permission for what she wanted to do.

They had had luncheon together, but to her relief not only Mr. Falkirk was present but also a man who was advising the Duke on improvements to the Castle.

They had ignored Tara as they talked of structural alterations, of renovations, roofing and damage.

Before Luncheon, the Duke had come into the Chieftain's Room and greeted her coldly. She thought he resented her being there, but she had no idea where else she might go.

It made her feel awkward and lost to have nothing to do. At the Orphanage the children would have been clinging to her and Mrs. Barrowfield ordering her around.

The Castle seemed quiet, empty and much too large, so that Tara felt as if every minute she grew smaller and smaller until she was in danger of disappearing.

Something rather frightening had happened at breakfast-time. She had gone to the Dining-Room at 8 o'clock to find only Mr. Falkirk was there.

"His Grace has gone riding," he explained. "He usually leaves the Castle soon after seven."

Tara was glad to be alone with Mr. Falkirk although they could not talk intimately as the servants were waiting on them.

But it was comforting to listen to his voice and know she had one friend in the Castle.

They had both finished and Mr. Falkirk was looking at his watch as if he had an appointment, when there was a noise and commotion outside the windows.

Mr. Falkirk moved towards one and Tara followed him.

Below they could see the Duke on his horse obviously just returned from his ride and in front of him there was a dirty ragged old woman.

She was shouting at him in a shrill voice, waving her bony arms as she did so, her white hair blowing in the wind around her wrinkled face.

"Who is that?" Tara asked.

"It is old Granny Beathag," Mr. Falkirk replied. "Fifty years ago she would have been burnt as a witch!"

"A witch!" Tara exclaimed.

The old woman was speaking a mixture of broad Scottish interspersed with Gaelic. Tara heard her utter the word *mallachd* several times.

"Surely *mallachd* means curse? I read it in one of your books."

Mr. Falkirk smiled.

"Granny Beathag has, I think, just heard of Duchess Margaret's death. She is reminding the Duke she warned him a year ago that if he married anyone but a McCraig the curse of the Clan would be on him and his wife."

"A curse," Tara whispered.

"Do not let it worry you," Mr. Falkirk laughed. "Every respectable Scottish family has a curse and a ghost! I will give you a book about them."

"But the Duchess has ... died, and the Clan must have cursed her."

"That is all nonsense," Mr. Falkirk said sharply. "Curses are but evil wishes said positively and Granny Beathag was only trying to work up feeling against the Kildonnons. An easy thing to do!"

"I am ... not a McCraig!"

"Now Tara!" Mr. Falkirk said soothingly, "you are too

intelligent to let the blathering of an old woman who is tetched in the head upset you."

He looked at her with a twinkle in his eye as he went on:

"For every curse Granny Beathag gives you, I will give you the very special blessing of the Falkirks. They are, I assure you, very much more effective!"

Tara tried to smile.

"The Duke is certainly not letting such maledictions trouble him!" Mr. Falkirk said.

He was looking out of the window as he spoke and Tara saw the Duke was laughing as he tossed a silver coin in the air towards the old woman.

She caught it deftly and turned to walk away, but Tara saw she was still shaking her head and muttering to herself.

When their meal, which was a short one, was over the visitor had asked that he should be taken up on the roof and the Duke had ordered Mr. Falkirk to escort him.

Tara had gone to her own room for her cloak and now she waited for the moment when she could attract the Duke's attention.

He raised his eyes from the letter he held in his hands and said sharply:

"What do you want?"

"I wonder, Your Grace ... if it would be ... all right for ... me to go for a ... walk?"

"For a walk? Why not?"

"I ... would like to do so if there ... is ... nothing else that you ... wish ... me to do."

"Do! What should you do?" he asked.

He glanced down at his letter again and then as she still stood there unsure and uncertain he said sharply:

"For God's sake get out and stay out! It must be obvious that I do not want you!"

There was both irritation and anger in his voice and he spoke with a violence that sounded to Tara like a clap of thunder.

She turned and ran down the stairs into the Hall. The

footman opened the door for her and she set off down the drive moving quickly as if the Duke's voice propelled her.

* * *

"Tea is ready, Your Grace," the Butler announced.

The Duke looked up from his desk at which he sat writing.

"Tell Mr. Falkirk I want him."

"Very good, Your Grace, but I think he is still with the gentleman who came to luncheon."

"Then tell him to come to me as soon as he is free."

"Very good, Your Grace."

It was half an hour later before Mr. Falkirk came into the Study.

"That man stayed a long time," the Duke remarked.

"I am afraid there is rather more to be done than we anticipated, Your Grace."

"That is nothing new!" the Duke answered.

He held up the letter he had been writing, towards his Comptroller.

"I have finished this letter to the Marquis of Stafford about his eviction of the Highlanders from Sutherland," he said. "I think you will approve of what I have said, but if you can make it any stronger, all the better."

"I will study it carefully."

"Let us have tea first," the Duke suggested.

He rose from his desk, walked across the landing and into the Chieftain's Room.

Tea was laid on a table on the hearth. There was a silver tray containing the tea-pot, the canister, the kettle, milk, cream, sugar and a strainer for the thin porcelain cups which had been brought over from France by one of the Duke's ancestors.

There were also plates of every sort of Scottish delicacy, including bread baked with sultanas, and hot scones in a silver covered dish which Mr. Falkirk thought were certain to delight Tara.

As if he also thought of her the Duke said sharply:

"Where is the Duchess? Surely she realises she should be here to pour out tea for me."

"I do not imagine anyone told her that was what you expected unless Your Grace did so?"

The Duke glared at Mr. Falkirk as if he was being impertinent before he said:

"Surely that is your job to tell my wife what times the meals are served?"

"I stand corrected, Your Grace. I will certainly take the responsibility for such matters in the future."

Unexpectedly the Duke laughed.

"All right, Falkirk, you win that skirmish."

He rang the bell — the same silver bell he had used the day before to summon Mr. Falkirk and Tara into the Chieftain's room. A servant appeared.

"Will you inform Her Grace that tea is ready?"

"Her Grace has not returned."

"Not returned!" the Duke exclaimed and added: "Of course, she went for a walk!"

He glanced at the clock over the mantelpiece.

"She has been gone for over three hours. She must be stronger, Falkirk, than you gave me to believe an orphan could be when you told me of the conditions in the Orphanage."

"I will make enquiries as to where Her Grace has gone," Mr. Falkirk said.

He walked from the Chieftain's room. The Duke picked up a scone from the table and eating it walked to the window.

In the Hall Mr. Falkirk questioned the servants on duty.

"Where did Her Grace go?"

"Straight down th' drive, Sir."

"She has not returned?"

"There's been not a sign of Her Grace since."

Mr. Falkirk looked out through the open door. It had been a day of sunshine, but now the sky had become overcast and he had the idea it might rain.

"Send for a horse from the stables!" he ordered.

It was brought round within a few minutes and a servant handed him his bonnet. Swinging himself into the saddle he set off down the drive.

When he reached the lodge gates he enquired of the Keeper if he had seen any sign of Tara and learnt that she had turned left up the Glen along the road over which they had travelled the day before.

Mr. Falkirk rode quite slowly in the direction pointed out to him, looking from side to side as he did so in case Tara might have taken to the moorland or wandered among the pine trees which grew down to the burn.

It was in fact a long time later and nearly three miles away from the Castle that finally he found her.

There were no trees and the moor seemed to stretch endlessly towards the horizon and he was in fact just thinking of turning back when he saw a dark figure on a patch of heather high above the road itself.

He had the feeling that she must have climbed, not to look at the view, but to see if there was a sign of a house or a habitat of any sort.

He turned his horse and rode up to her silently to find her crying helplessly, her hands over her face as she crouched amongst the heather.

Mr. Falkirk dismounted, leaving his horse to crop what grass he could find. He stood looking down at Tara and then as she went on crying he sat down beside her.

"What is the matter? What has upset you?" he asked.

She raised her face at the sound of his voice and then as if she could not help herself she turned towards him and went on crying against his shoulder.

His arms went round her and he held her protectively.

"It is all right," he said quietly. "Tell me all about it, it cannot be as bad as that."

"It ... is ... worse!" Tara sobbed. "He told me to go ... out and ... stay ... out. And I have ... no ... where to ... go and ... no money."

Her last words were choked by her tears and now she cried tempestuously as a child might do so.

Mr. Falkirk drew in his breath.

"It is all right, Tara," he said. "His Grace did not mean it. He was angry but not with you."

"He married me out of ... revenge! He does not ... want

... me and now he has had ... his ... revenge I must ... go ... away."

Mr. Falkirk looked out over the moorland as if the beauty of it would help him choose his words.

"I am afraid, Tara, it is not as easy as that."

"Easy?" she questioned.

"You see, my dear," Mr. Falkirk said slowly, "every action we commit has long consequences which unfortunately affect not only ourselves but other people."

She was listening to him but she knew she did not understand what he was trying to say.

"I am going to break a confidence," Mr. Falkirk said, "and tell you now why the Duke is angry and why he brought you to the Castle to become his wife."

"It was to ... hurt the Kildonnons ... I realise ... that."

"What you do not know," Mr. Falkirk said, "is why he wanted to hurt them."

"I have ... wondered what it ... was."

"It is not my story but I feel that because you are now the Duchess of Arkcraig, it is something you should know."

Tara put her head against his shoulder and his arm was still around her.

He thought that this was how he would like to sit with his daughter if he had one. He felt as if Tara was in fact as near to him as any child of his own could be and just as dear.

He chose his words very simply. He told her how the Duke's wife had hated him because he was a McCraig; how she had loved her cousin, Neil Kildonnon; and how eventually they had run away to France together.

He told her of the duel, at which he had been present; how the Duke had taken every possible care to see it was conducted in an honourable manner and was the same type of duel that had been fought by gentlemen all through the centuries.

"But he ... killed ... him!" Tara whispered.

"Neil Kildonnon died of his wounds. That is a very different thing."

"And the ... Duchess?"

94

Again deliberately under-playing the drama of it, Mr. Falkirk told how the Duchess had stabbed herself and how although everything had been done to save her from the results of the laudanum she had died.

After he had finished speaking there was a long silence and then Tara said :

"Was ... she ... very ... beautiful?"

"Most people thought her attractive, or very bonny, as we should say in this part of the world."

"The Duke ... loved her?"

"To tell the truth," he replied with a faint smile, "I do not think His Grace has ever been really in love. There have been many women in his life, but if he has loved anyone it has been his Clan."

"Now he is ... hurt and ... unhappy."

"His pride is hurt – and the pride of a McCraig is a very strong and violent emotion. It will take him time to get over what he is suffering and that, Tara, is where you have to help him."

"How?"

"You are his wife."

"I never imagined ... I never dreamt that ... this was what was waiting for me ... in ... Scotland."

"No, nor did I. But it happened and you cannot run away. It is your responsibility, it is your duty and, if you like, it is the cause in which you must believe and for which you must fight."

Tara drew in her breath.

"As the Scots fought for what they ... believed to be ... right."

"Exactly!"

Tara wiped the tears from her cheeks.

"I would not have you ... think me a ... coward. I will come ... back."

"I thought you would," Mr. Falkirk answered.

*　　*　　*

The Duke was in his Study attending to a large pile of correspondence that had been waiting for him on his return from France, when Mr. Falkirk came into the room.

He shut the door behind him and moved to stand in front of the desk.

After a moment the Duke looked up at him.

"Where have you been?" he enquired. "I wondered what had happened to you."

"Do you remember," Mr. Falkirk asked, "when you were about sixteen thrashing a man who was much larger and stronger than you because you learnt he had been cruel to his dog?"

"Yes, of course I remember!" the Duke exclaimed. "He was a shepherd and he drank too much. The dog had been so ill-treated it had to be destroyed. But after I dealt with him I doubt if that man would ever beat a dog again!"

"You came back to the Castle after you had finished with him," Mr. Falkirk said, "and you told me that you loathed cruelty of any sort and that you would fight any man whoever he might be, should you find him behaving in such a manner towards an animal."

"I recall my anger and my disgust," the Duke said. "What are you saying, Falkirk? Are you telling me that somebody on the Estate is behaving in a similar manner. Because I will not have it?"

"Not on the Estate, Your Grace, in the Castle!"

The Duke was about to speak but Mr. Falkirk went on:

"I found the Duchess nearly three miles away crying helplessly in the heather because she had nowhere to go and no money."

"Good God!"

"You told her to leave – at least that is the way she interpreted it. She is used to orders and to obeying them."

The Duke rose from his desk.

"I had no idea! I did not mean to upset her. She interrupted me when I was reading a most infuriating letter from my Aunt Harriet who had heard some vague rumour that Margaret had gone to France and was taking me to task for not giving her a child."

He paused.

"I dislike busy-bodies!"

"So do I," Mr. Falkirk said. "But the Duchess is rather different from any woman Your Grace will have met before."

The Duke walked across the room to stand looking out of the window and Mr. Falkirk had the feeling that he was looking inward at himself.

After some minutes had passed he said:

"I was so blind with rage that in marrying her I acted impulsively without actually envisaging the consequences. I suppose it is too late to send her back?"

"Much too late, Your Grace. She is your wife!"

The Duke gave a deep sigh which seemed to come from the very depths of his being.

"I have got myself into a mess, Falkirk. I suppose you cannot pull me out of it as you have done so often in the past?"

"I am afraid this is something you have to do yourself, Your Grace."

There was a long silence. Then the Duke said:

"Where is the Duchess now?"

"I suggested she should lie down," Mr. Falkirk said, "and told Mrs. McCraig to take her some tea."

"She will dine with me?"

"I am sure she will."

"Then I will try, Falkirk, to behave in a more civilised manner."

"I am certain you will not find it difficult, Your Grace."

Mr. Falkirk walked towards the door. As he reached it without turning round the Duke said very quietly:

"Thank you, Falkirk."

Chapter Five

Climbing up the side of the moor with the wind on her face and the grouse moving ahead of them, Tara thought it was the most exciting thing she had ever done in her life.

She could hardly believe what she had heard when during luncheon the Duke had said:

"Would you like to climb to the cairn on the top of Ben Ark this afternoon? There is the finest view in the whole of Scotland and one can see for hundreds of miles."

For a moment she stared at him wide-eyed, hardly believing that he was giving her an invitation. Then she replied:

"Can I ... really do that?"

"I am prepared to take you if you wish to go."

"It will be wonderful!" Tara exclaimed.

From the moment she had come from her bed-room last night to join the Duke for dinner in the Chieftain's Room, he had behaved quite differently from before.

When she had left Mr. Falkirk she had been ashamed of her own behaviour and thought how foolish she had been to run away just because the Duke was cross with her.

But it was all part of the fear she had felt the night before when she had waited for him in the huge bed-room and unaccountably he had not come.

She did not know when she had fallen asleep, but had awoken in what she thought must be the early hours of the morning.

The fire had died down and there was only the barest glimmer from the ashes.

Hardly aware of what she was doing, Tara had stumbled towards the bed and climbed into it to fall asleep until she was awakened to find the curtains drawn back and the maids bringing cans of hot water.

She had not realised that the velvet cover from the bed had been laid over her while she slept and that the Duke had come and gone away again.

When they were together at luncheon, Tara had thought that she had been foolish to be so afraid of him, realising he was in fact younger and much less awe-inspiring than she had felt at first.

He talked to her quite naturally and asked her about herself. She told him of the books she was reading which Mr. Falkirk had lent her.

"You will find plenty of books in the Library," the Duke said, "but many of them were bought by my Grandfather, and I think you would find them heavy and exceedingly dull."

"It is so exciting to have a book of any sort to read that I cannot imagine I would ever find one too dull to finish."

The Duke had smiled and Tara had added:

"May I really borrow the books from your Library?"

"With the greatest of pleasure," he answered.

She gave a little sigh.

"Everything is so exciting here. I had a wedding-present today!"

"A wedding-present?" the Duke queried.

"It was from Janet, one of the maids who look after me. Her Grandmother distills the fragrance from the heather and makes it into a perfume. She brought me a bottle."

She thought the Duke looked surprised and said a little nervously:

"Was I wrong to accept it? Perhaps I should give it back?"

"No, of course not," he answered quickly. "It was just that I was surprised that Janet should be so thoughtful and I so forgetful. I suppose you will be thinking it very remiss of me that I have not given you a present."

"Why should I think such a thing?" Tara exclaimed. "There is no reason why anyone should give me a present; in fact I have never had one before and the bottle of scent was so exciting."

"Never had a present before?" the Duke said slowly.

He sounded so astonished that Tara could not help laughing.

"Of course not, in an Orphanage!"

She saw the incredulity in his eyes as she went on:

"When I had time I used to make little dolls out of rags that were not wanted for the small children, but the boys never had anything to play with. I think that is one of the reasons they were always fighting each other."

"When we go to London," the Duke said, "you will yourself be able to take presents to the Orphanage."

Tara stared at him.

"Do you mean that?"

"Of course I mean it."

She thought for a moment and then she said:

"It would be ... expensive if you were to give ... every child a toy."

"Perhaps it would be best if the money was spent on you. Then only one present would be necessary."

She looked at him hastily and she had a feeling he was looking at her strangely, almost as if he was testing her.

"I want nothing," she said. "But for the children of the Orphanage to have toys would be the most exciting thing in the world, both for them and for me."

"Then you really need nothing for yourself?"

"Only books," Tara answered, 'and you have already told me I can have those."

She thought there was a strange expression on the Duke's face as he turned the conversation to other subjects.

It was as interesting having him explain things to her as it had been to listen to Mr. Falkirk, but because he spoke more quickly and there was a kind of vitality in all he said, it seemed to Tara that everything they discussed had a sparkle to which she responded.

Then as the meal was ending the Duke had suggested that they should climb to the cairn.

She could hardly believe that he really meant it until they set off walking, not down the drive, but through the gardens and shrubberies.

Beyond these there was a twisting path, little more than a

sheep track, which led directly towards Ben Ark which towered above the Glen.

They had not gone very far before Tara realised it was extremely hot, as was to be expected in July.

But it was a hard and fast rule at the Orphanage, set down by the Duchess Harriet, that no girl should leave the premises without wearing the heavy black cloak which covered her grey cotton gown.

Therefore without thinking, without even questioning that it would prove cumbersome and overheating in the July sunshine, Tara had put on her cloak.

When they had climbed so high that the Castle was far beneath them, the Duke turned to say:

"It is very warm now, but you will find it cool when we reach the summit."

"I am rather hot," Tara admitted, "but if I am lagging behind, Your Grace, it is because I have to keep stopping to look at the beauty of the moors. And I have just found a piece of white heather."

"You will find plenty more," the Duke said, "but why do you not take off your cloak?"

"Can I do that?"

"Why not?" he said, "there is no-one to object except the grouse."

She laughed a little shyly and then unclasped her cloak at the neck.

"As a matter of fact I think I will join you by taking off my jacket," he said. "I was wise enough to leave my plaid behind."

He took off his jacket as he spoke and Tara saw beneath it he was wearing a thin lawn shirt which made a sharp contrast to the top of his pleated kilt encircling his waist.

"That is better," he said in a tone of relief, "and now we had better go on climbing. There is a long way yet to go, but it will be very much easier coming down."

Tara was sure of that, but she was in fact not tired.

She felt as if everything that was happening was so new and thrilling that it gave her an energy she had never had before.

Up and up they went until just above them Tara could see the cairn, which the Duke had told her before they started off was made of stones carried laboriously up the hill by the Clansmen and placed on the summit in memory of his Great-Great-Grandfather.

"It became a watch-tower and in the olden days there was always a man beside it on the look-out for our enemies," he explained.

"How did he signal to the Clans when they were approaching?" Tara enquired.

"He would light a fire," the Duke answered. "In the daytime the smoke rising from it would alert the Clansmen and at night the flames would shine in the darkness."

"It must have been very cold for the man keeping guard there in the winter when there was snow on the hills."

"The McCraigs were tough in those days," the Duke replied with a smile. "It is only recently that we are becoming used to comforts and soft living which sap our strength."

Tara could not help thinking that for many of the Scots their lives were still hard and comfortless, but she had no wish to argue with the Duke, only to learn from him.

As she followed him up the twisting track she thought there was so much he could tell her and so many questions she wanted to ask.

'I must be careful not to bore him,' she thought humbly.

At the same time almost instinctively she lessened the distance between them.

"We are nearly there," the Duke said over his shoulder. "I have brought my spy-glass so you will be able to see further than you have ever seen before in your life."

There were now only a few steps from the cairn which, silhouetted against the sky, was much larger than it had seemed from the valley.

As he spoke the Duke looked down to where he had attached his spy-glass by a strap to his side and because he was not looking ahead it was Tara who saw that a man had suddenly appeared from behind the cairn.

With a violent sense of shock she saw he had a gun in his hands.

He pointed it straight at the Duke and as he did so Tara screamed.

It was her scream which saved the Duke's life. He turned round and the bullet which should have hit him straight in the heart, caught him sideways on the arm.

But the impact threw him off balance and he fell, hitting his head as he did so on the cairn.

Tara was paralysed where she stood. Now the Duke had fallen she was looking straight at the man who had shot him.

She recognised him immediately as one of the Kildonnons who had been in the Chieftain's Room when she was married.

He too stared at her.

Then he turned and started running down the other side of the mountain, his kilt swinging out with every movement and there was no mistaking the green and yellow of his tartan.

Tara ran to the Duke and knelt down beside him.

The blood from his arm already flowed over his white shirt in a crimson tide and she saw also that he was bleeding at the side of his forehead where there was a deep gash where he had struck a pointed stone.

Another woman might have panicked, but Tara was used to accidents.

The Duke's jacket was on the ground beside him and from it she took his handkerchief and tied it tightly round his arm to stop the bleeding.

Then she drew his skean-dhu from his leg and slit his linen shirt from the cuff to the shoulder to lay bare the wound from the gun.

For a moment she stared at it in consternation. She realised that the bullet would be somewhere in the torn flesh but the blood made it difficult for her to see very clearly.

Because she knew it was the right thing to do she tied the handkerchief even tighter, and then she wondered what she could use as a bandage.

She saw that the Duke possessed nothing suitable except

his handkerchief which she had already used.

Then turning her back on him she lifted her grey skirt and with the skean-dhu in her hand tried to cut away a piece of her white calico petticoat.

It was difficult and as she was doing it a sudden thought came to her. Mr. Falkirk knew where they had gone for he had seen them before they left the Castle.

"I am taking the Duchess to the cairn at the top of Ben Ark," the Duke had said.

Mr. Falkirk smiled.

"It is a long walk and will do Her Grace good after so many days in a coach. I think before we arrived we were both feeling as if we might lose the use of our legs."

"If they ache tonight I have no intention of taking the blame!" the Duke replied lightly.

Mr. Falkirk watched them as they set off across the garden.

When they did not return Tara knew he would surely send someone in search of them, but that meant the Duke would be without proper attention for a long time.

She was well aware that the bullet should be extracted as quickly as possible.

As modestly as possible she untied her petticoat which slipped to the ground. Stepping out of it she first hacked away a wide piece of the calico which she could use as a bandage and then she tied what remained onto the long stick which the Duke had carried in his hand as he climbed the hill.

Mr. Falkirk had told her that every Chieftain carried a walnut stick and it was symbolic of the crook that was the sign of a shepherd.

"A Chieftain leads and protects his Clan in the same way," Mr. Falkirk had explained.

Tara pressed the stick into the soft ground beside the cairn, and as the Duke had foretold there was a wind which lifted her petticoat so that it floated out like a flag.

She felt someone at the Castle or perhaps one of the keepers who she knew were always on the moors, would see it.

Then she knelt down beside the Duke to put the bandage on his arm but as she did so she realised that she must have a pad of some sort.

She had learnt when the boys in the Orphanage fought each other with knives that it was no use bandaging their wounds unless she put a thick pad on them first.

She wondered what she could use and then pulled her ugly grey cap from her head.

She rolled it into a ball, covered it with her own handkerchief and made a very effective pad. Then she placed it on the Duke's wound and bandaged his arm with a long strip of calico from her petticoat.

She knew that she must not leave the handkerchief which was preventing the flow of blood on his arm too long and while she was trying to gauge how long it had been there she looked carefully at his forehead.

She realised it was his fall that had rendered him unconscious. He had struck a jagged stone and she was certain that it would result in concussion.

He was lying sprawled uncomfortably half against the cairn, his legs doubled under him, but she knew he was too large and too heavy for her to move him.

She looked back down the valley, hoping that she would see someone coming to their rescue, and as she did so rain began pouring down from a suddenly darkening sky.

Hastily Tara threw the Duke's jacket over him and put her own cloak round her shoulders.

The warmth of the climb up had been succeeded by sudden cold, and the rain beating on her face had a sharp chill about it which made her apprehensive for the Duke.

He had lost a lot of blood and she knew from long experience that this meant he would soon feel cold and shivery.

"I must keep him warm," she told herself.

She wished they were lower down the mountain and not on the very summit, but there was nothing she could do about that.

She thought perhaps she should take off her cloak and cover the Duke with it completely.

Then she had a better idea.

She sat down with her back to the cairn and by exerting all her strength managed to pull the Duke into her arms. She held him as she had held so often at the Orphanage, children that were hurt.

She pulled her cloak round him so that while the rain beat down on her head his body was protected and dry.

There was nothing she could do about his legs, bare from the top of his hose to above his knee. But she felt perhaps they were tougher than any other part of his anatomy.

She wished she had something to put round his forehead, but her handkerchief and her petticoat had both been fully utilised.

The gash was bleeding and was marking the bodice of her dress but it was not the flow of crimson blood which had come from his arm.

"I wonder how long we shall have to wait," Tara murmured.

Then she thought how extraordinary it was that she, an orphan, who was of no consequence whatsoever, should be sitting on top of a mountain with one of the most important men of Scotland in her arms.

"He is unconscious and will never know I held him like this," she told herself. "It is the only way I can keep him warm."

The rain seemed to grow heavier and then as suddenly as it had come from the skies it ceased. A watery sun came out and with it there was a rainbow over the Glen.

Tara felt it was almost a divine message from Heaven itself. Never had she imagined anything could be so beautiful, so ethereal and mystic.

It seemed as if it brought her a message, although what it was she had no idea.

She only knew that the sheer loveliness of it seemed to lift her heart and sweep away the fear that had lurked within her ever since she had come to the Castle.

'I am sure it means that everything will be all right, not only for me but for the Duke,' she thought and remembered the curse.

Mr. Falkirk had laughed at the old woman, but Tara could not help thinking that the Duke had already encountered exceptionally bad luck.

He had been unfortunate in his marriage, and now he had nearly lost his life.

She wondered what she would have done if he had been shot through the heart as his assailant had intended and she had found herself alone with a dead man – who was her husband.

When she had gone to bed last night she had not been so apprehensive as she had been the night before, because some instinct told her that the Duke would not come to her room.

She did not know why she was so certain of this.

Perhaps it was the way in which he said good-night and told her 'to sleep well'; perhaps it was because the huge bed-room did not now seem so awesome and she had not been too afraid to get into bed.

"He has suffered so much," she told herself, "that he feels as if everyone is his enemy."

And she thought that that was what he felt about her, even though she had been brought to the Castle on his own instigation.

"I do not think revenge ever makes people happy," she decided.

She thought now that if the Duke had been killed the ensuing warfare between the McCraigs and the Kildonnons would be so bitter and violent, that doubtless hundreds of them would lose their lives.

She thought again of the man who had shot the Duke and was quite certain it was the Kildonnon whom she had heard him address as Rory.

He had seemed the eldest of the young men, and the hatred that had seemed to exude from him towards the Duke, almost like a living flame, had been so intense that Tara had felt it vibrate on the air.

She had known too that when he had taken her hand in homage he had hated her too and there had been a smouldering fury in his eyes which had made her tremble.

Now he had had his revenge! Perhaps he had been watching them coming up the hill-side waiting until the right moment when he could shoot the Duke full in the chest.

He would have been a murderer, while she would have been the only witness who could identify the criminal.

'If I tell them the truth now,' she thought, 'the McCraigs will rise in fury and attack the Kildonnons.'

She could almost hear in her mind the bagpipes calling them to arms; hear the sound of their hurrying feet as they sped over the border with their guns in their hands to take their revenge on the Kildonnons.

"Somehow I must prevent that," she told herself. "The Duke is alive and that is all that matters."

She held him a little closer and then put up one hand to wipe the wet hair from her forehead.

*   *   *

"I doubt if His Grace will regain consciousness until tomorrow or maybe later," the Doctor said.

He was a red-faced cheerful man who had removed the bullet from the Duke's arm skilfully but at the same time so roughly that Tara was thankful the patient was not in a position to know anything about it.

"His Grace fell against the cairn?" the Doctor asked as he examined the wound on the Duke's forehead.

"Yes, he crashed down against it," Tara answered.

"It's a nasty place," the Doctor said, "but if we keep it clean, there'll not be much harm done, though undoubtedly it'll leave a scar."

"I do not think His Grace will worry about that," Mr. Falkirk said, "but when he awakes he will find it extremely painful."

"He will indeed," the Doctor agreed. "He'll have a bad head on him and doubtless it will ache for a wee while, but that'll not trouble a McCraig."

"And His Grace's arm?" Mr. Falkirk enquired.

"That will heal, but it'll take time and he must do as little as possible. Keep him in bed if you can."

The Doctor laughed and added:

"I know His Grace of old and he's a difficult patient!

He'll never obey anyone, least of all his Doctor!"

He put a hand against the Duke's forehead where it was not bruised.

"He may develop a fever," he continued, "but he's in good health as he always is. It should not last long."

"What about nursing?" Mr. Falkirk enquired.

The Doctor put a hand up to his chin.

"There, you have me, Mr. Falkirk. I think you'll have to find someone in the Castle to take care of His Grace. There's no-one in the village I can recommend."

"I will nurse him," Tara said quietly.

Both the Doctor and Mr. Falkirk looked at her in surprise.

She looked very young with her red curls rioting over her head and very different from the motherly sort of woman they were envisaging as a nurse.

The Doctor voiced the doubts that were in both men's minds.

"Do you know about nursing, Lassie? ... I mean Your Grace."

From the moment of meeting Tara he had found it difficult to realise that she was the new Duchess.

Tara smiled.

"I have nursed boys with broken legs, broken arms, and worse bruises on their foreheads than the Duke has at the moment."

She saw a look of surprise in the Doctor's eyes.

"I have also had twenty-two children down with measles at the same time, some of them running a very high fever, and I managed without any help."

"Where can you have had all this experience?" the Doctor enquired.

"Her Grace has worked amongst the poor in London," Mr. Falkirk said quickly before Tara could speak.

"Then His Grace is in good hands," the Doctor replied.

It was in fact Mr. Falkirk who organised everything.

He decided that Tara should nurse the Duke at night and Hector, His Grace's valet, during the day, or at least until such time that she had not only had some sleep but walked in the fresh air.

Mr. Falkirk had a couch carried into the Duke's bedroom so that Tara could lie down during the night.

She was relieved at six o'clock in the morning when Hector came on duty and she would then go into her own room to get into bed and sleep deeply and dreamlessly.

She had at first been rather frightened when the Duke did not quickly regain consciousness; yet she could not help thinking that it was a good thing that he was not aware of his swollen and inflamed arm.

She had to change the bandages two or three times during the night and the Doctor came twice a day to do the same.

"Surely he should have come round by now?" she asked Mr. Falkirk on the second day when she joined him in the Chieftain's Room.

"There has been no change," he replied. "Hector says he is very restless, tossing from side to side."

"He was like that last night," Tara said, "and I am sure he has a high temperature."

"I expect his head is hurting him, perhaps more than his arm," Mr. Falkirk said. "I remember when I had concussion I was aware of pain although I had no idea of where I was or what had happened to me."

That night when Tara was alone with the Duke she sat down beside the bed and started to massage his forehead very gently.

He had been moving from side to side but after her fingers had been touching him for a little time he grew quieter.

'Perhaps I am magicking the pain away,' she thought, remembering that was what the children had called her massage.

Then because her arm ached from the angle at which she was sitting, she sat down on the top of the bed and pulled the Duke into the same position in which she had held him when they were on the mountainside.

From the moment she had begun nursing him, in fact from the moment after he had been shot, she had found it difficult to think of him as the awe-inspiring, terrifying husband who had married her in his desire to avenge himself on the Kildonnons.

In fact, he had become just like one of the boys in the Orphanage, who once they were hurt and injured ceased to be tough and aggressive and became only small children who wanted a mother to console them.

Since she was the only available substitute she had done her best not only to take away the pain but also to instil in them a little of the courage which she knew they would need in the future.

Terrible tales of how apprentices were ill-treated by unscrupulous employers were often whispered round the Orphanage.

Tara had begged Mrs. Barrowfield to be careful of the men who demanded orphans as if they were just pieces of merchandise without any feelings or personalities of their own.

Sometimes when the boys she was fond of left, white-faced and frightened of the unknown, she would cry when they were gone, wishing she could protect them from what she sensed would be a hard and hostile world.

She felt in the same way she must protect the Duke, not only from physical pain but from the emotional suffering he had endured.

She felt it flowed like poison running through his veins, changing him and altering his character.

On the third night the Duke regained consciousness.

Tara was lying beside him and was massaging his forehead with her fingers when suddenly he opened his eyes and said:

"I am – thirsty."

For a moment she felt as if she could not have heard him.

Then gently she took her arm from around his neck and laid him back against the pillow.

"I will get you a drink," she said.

She climbed down from the high bed to fetch a glass of Barley-water. She lifted his head very gently and held the glass to his lips.

"Are you hungry?" she asked. "I have some warm soup in a hay-box. If you could swallow a little of it, I think it would give you strength."

He looked at her as if it was hard to understand what she was saying. Then he asked:

"What – has – happened?"

"You had an accident."

"Where?"

"By the cairn. You fell against a sharp stone which hurt your head."

"I – remember."

The Duke shut his eyes and she thought he had gone to sleep again. She stood looking down at him not liking to lie on the couch in case he should need her.

Two hours later he asked:

"Why are – you here?"

"I am trying to get you well," Tara answered. "The Doctor is very pleased with you."

"Someone – shot me?"

"Yes, I know, but it was an accident."

"Who was it?"

"I did not see him," Tara said. "I was too busy worrying about you."

Now she insisted on the Duke having a few spoonfuls of the nourishing beef and venison soup which had been kept hot in a hay-box by the fire-place.

"No – more," he said.

"Please try one more spoonful," she begged, "it will make you strong. I have been so worried about you lying here with nothing to eat."

She put the spoon against his lips and he swallowed the soup, then shut his eyes as if he was determined to take no more.

Tara left when Hector came on duty but she found it difficult to rest. At noon she went again to the Duke's room.

"I washed His Grace and shaved him," Hector said. "He had a little to eat and has now fallen asleep."

"I will go outside for a few minutes," Tara told him, "and come back when I return."

She went along towards the Chieftain's Room and as she reached it she realised there were several people coming up the stairs.

To her astonishment she saw it was The Kildonnon and with him were his two elder sons. Escorting them was Mr.

Falkirk and Tara thought that he looked at her in a manner that was almost one of warning.

"The Kildonnon has called to see you," he said to Tara.

"To see me!" Tara exclaimed in surprise.

"Yes, Duchess," The Kildonnon said.

They moved into the Chieftain's Room and Mr. Falkirk shut the door.

"I have learnt," The Kildonnon began, "that, although everyone has been told it was an accident, the Duke was actually shot by someone on Ben Ark when you and he had climbed to the summit of it."

Tara was looking at The Kildonnon and she realised that Mr. Falkirk's eyes were also on his face.

"I want the truth, Duchess!" The Kildonnon said. "You were there and you must have seen the Duke's assassin. If it was one of my sons, as I suspect, I would rather learn the truth now than when the McCraigs begin to take their revenge upon us."

He spoke harshly and Tara drew in her breath. This was what she had known would happen.

"I am afraid you have been misinformed, Sir," she said after a moment. "The Duke was wounded by an accident that occurred when he was carrying his own gun. He stumbled, fell heavily onto a jagged rock, his gun went off and wounded him in the arm."

"Are you sure that is what occurred?" The Kildonnon enquired.

"I was there," Tara replied. "I expect you have heard that the Duke was rendered unconscious, not from the wound in his arm, but from his fall against the cairn."

She clasped her hands together as she went on :

"We had a terrible time getting His Grace down from the mountain. Fortunately one of the keepers saw the signal I had put up to show we were in trouble, and when he found the Duke unconscious he fetched a number of men to carry him home on an improvised stretcher."

She gave a faint smile as she said :

"I was terrified all the while in case they should drop His Grace, but fortunately they were strong men."

"That is exactly what happened," Mr. Falkirk agreed. "But we appreciate, Kildonnon, your coming here to find out the truth for yourself."

As the Chief turned to talk to him Tara met the eyes of Rory Kildonnon. He was looking at her, she knew, in a kind of wonderment as if he had steeled himself in the expectation of her saying something very different.

Tara looked back at him and thought he understood why she had lied. Then The Kildonnon said:

"Will you convey to His Grace, Duchess, my sincere hopes for a quick recovery."

"I am sure he will be very grateful for your concern," Tara answered.

"And may we hope that when he is better you will *both* visit us?"

She knew by the way he spoke and the expression in his eyes that her story had not deceived him. But he was grateful, as she was sure Rory Kildonnon was grateful.

When the Kildonnons, refusing any refreshment, had left the Castle, Mr. Falkirk said with a smile:

"The keepers will be looking everywhere for the gun with which His Grace managed to wound himself."

"Then you had better make sure they find one!" Tara said.

Mr. Falkirk laughed then said seriously:

"I could not believe anyone would have such a quick understanding of how explosive such a situation might have been, had it not been for your very convincing explanation of an accident."

"I knew that was what you would want," Tara said, "and I think His Grace would want it too."

"I hope he will," Mr. Falkirk said quietly.

It was late that evening, when Tara thought the Duke was asleep, that she crept across the bedroom to put a log on the fire and as she turned saw by the light of the flames that his eyes were open.

"Hector tells me that The Kildonnon called today," he said.

"Hector should not trouble you with gossip," Tara

answered. "It is important for you to get well and not to worry about anything."

"Why did he come here?"

Tara was still for a moment. Then she said:

"He wished to enquire after your health."

"What else?"

"He thought that someone had shot you by the cairn and I think he imagined it was one of his sons."

"And was it?"

"I was ... looking the ... other way."

"But you must have seen who pulled the trigger?"

There was a pause before Tara said:

"I told The Kildonnon it was an accident, that you stumbled and hit your head against the cairn and the gun you were carrying went off by accident."

"And he believed that!"

"He wanted to believe it, just as we want to ... believe it."

"And you think I intend to accept this murderous attempt upon my life without making any effort of retaliation?"

"It would be very easy to incite the McCraigs to take their revenge on the Kildonnons," Tara said. "But is that really what you want?"

"Why should I want anything else?"

"Because you are too important, too big to belittle yourself by stupid feuds, by revenging yourself on a boy who himself was seeking revenge."

Tara made a little gesture with her hands.

"It would go on for ever as it has in the past. I have been making Mr. Falkirk tell me about the history of the McCraigs, and it seems to me there has been far too much fighting and not enough thinking!"

Tara spoke the thoughts that had been in her mind and only when she had actually uttered them did she realise how rude and impertinent they sounded. She looked at the Duke apprehensively.

"I am sorry, Your Grace, if I was rude," she said humbly. "It is just that I am afraid of bloodshed; afraid of other Kildonnons trying to kill you. And as you cannot walk about wearing armour, one day they will succeed!"

She drew in her breath before she added:

"Then the feud will go on and on until they are all killed, and perhaps their children and your children. The whole thing is so tragically unnecessary!"

The Duke did not speak and after a moment she said:

"I could not ask Your Grace what you ... wanted me to say, but I felt you would not ... wish either your people or the Kildonnons to know the ... real truth."

"Then you are prepared to let Rory Kildonnon get off scot-free!"

"You knew it was he!"

"He is the only one likely to have the guts to try to kill me," the Duke said.

"He was afraid when he came here today," Tara said. "Afraid I would denounce him and of the consequences. And The Kildonnon was afraid too."

"So you sent them home happy with the thought that I am such a fool I cannot handle a gun!" the Duke said scathingly.

"They knew perfectly well what the true story was," Tara replied. "They asked me if when you were well enough we would ... *both* visit them."

There was silence and then the Duke said:

"Are you sure that is what he asked?"

"Yes, and he ... meant it."

"I have a feeling," the Duke said slowly, "that you have begun a new chapter, Tara, in the history of the Mc-Craigs."

* * *

The Duke walked slowly but with dignity down the passage to the Chieftain's Room.

Mr. Falkirk went ahead of him and pulled forward a comfortable chair in which he could seat himself as soon as he reached it.

The Butler hurried forward with a glass of wine on a silver tray. The Duke raised it to his lips and took a few sips before he said:

"I feel stronger than I thought I would."

"One always feels weak the first time one gets up after

an illness," Mr. Falkirk said, "and putting on clothes is a tremendous effort."

The Duke smiled.

"You are very sympathetic, Falkirk. It makes me furious to feel as weak as a purling babe."

"You will soon be strong again. And you must thank your wife for her care of you."

"I am well aware who else I have to be grateful to," the Duke said, "and you are one of them."

Mr. Falkirk looked at him in surprise.

"You must be worse than I thought to be thanking me, Your Grace. You usually are bawling me out for something I have omitted to do, when you have been unable to attend to it yourself."

"Am I such a monster?" the Duke said.

"Not half as bad as your Father was," Mr. Falkirk replied.

The Duke laughed.

"Your compliments overwhelm me. As I have often said, Falkirk, I shall never grow conceited while you are about. You are far too conscious of my faults."

"And very proud of your virtues," Mr. Falkirk said quietly.

The two men smiled at each other. Ever since the Duke was a young boy, Mr. Falkirk had been there to help him, to guide him and at times to cover up for him.

He always felt that his Comptroller was far closer to him than any of his relatives and he was in fact much fonder of him.

At that moment there was a sound of voices outside the Chieftain's Room.

"Visitors!" the Duke said sharply. "For God's sake, Falkirk, I have no wish to see anyone!"

Mr. Falkirk moved towards the door but he was too late. It opened and a resplendent figure came into the room.

It was a man of about forty wearing a kilt which because he was wearing it seemed to have a sophisticated elegance that was very personal.

"Charles!" the Duke's exclamation was a cry of welcome.

"Hullo, Heron," the new-comer replied. "I expected to find you in bed at death's door from all the stories I have been hearing."

"Then you have been told a lot of lies."

"I am glad I did not believe them, but I see your arm is in a sling."

"I will tell you all about it, but first, have something to drink?" the Duke said. "Falkirk, you remember my cousin Charles?"

"Of course," Mr. Falkirk replied. "It is good to see you, My Lord."

"You look just the same, you old rascal! Still slogging along with these countrified McCraigs? I have told you that I have a job for you any time you wish to leave them."

Mr. Falkirk smiled, this was on old joke.

"I have the uncomfortable feeling, My Lord, I shall leave my bones among them."

"But not for many years!" the visitor replied.

He sat down by the Duke.

"Now, Heron, what have you been up to?" he asked. "There are the most wild rumours circulating the country-side."

"What sort of rumours?" the Duke asked.

"That Margaret is dead for one!"

"That is true."

"Good God! And I heard a whisper yesterday on my way here that you had married again."

"That also is true."

"Then it is certainly time I paid you a visit. I am completely out of date with your very tangled affairs and insist on being put into the picture of all that is occurring!"

He paused because the Butler was presenting him with a glass of champagne.

"I would rather it was whisky!" he said, "but I suppose I must drink your health, Heron. You will have to hurry and get well if you are coming to Edinburgh."

"Why should I want to do that?"

"Good Lord, do you know nothing in this backwater! The King is paying us a visit!"

"What King?"

"The King of England, Scotland, Ireland and Wales! What other King is there? And incidentally, Heron, he is a damn good fellow and I think you will like him."

"My dear Charles, if you like to hang about Courts I shall make no effort to stop you, but all that pomp and circumstance bores me stiff. Besides I have a lot to do here!"

"You cannot say that! It is one of the most important things that have ever happened, that George IV should actually be making an official visit to Edinburgh."

"I suppose that is the reason that you condescended to visit us."

"His Majesty sent me ahead, not to spy out the land, but to make sure the red carpets were down. He likes applause and is insistent that he should be well and truly welcomed."

"When does he arrive?"

"On the 15th August."

"That gives you fifteen days," the Duke said. "Are you going to stay with me over the Sabbath?"

"No, I must get back to Edinburgh, but I will stay the night."

"Good!"

Mr. Falkirk was just leaving the room as the Duke called out:

"The Earl of Strathairdrie will stay the night. See to his entourage. I expect there is a whole cavalcade of them outside."

Mr. Falkirk smiled.

"Leave it to me, Your Grace."

The Earl of Strathairdrie leant back in his chair and took another sip of his champagne before he said:

"I have been rather worried about you, Heron."

"Why?" the Duke asked.

"Because I felt from the very beginning that your marriage would be a mistake."

"I remember your warning me against it!"

"These idealistic schemes are all right on paper, but in practice they do not work. You never cared for Margaret and it was quite obvious what her feelings were for you."

"I suppose I was conceited enough to think she would find me at least a tolerable husband."

"A lot of women have found you more than tolerable, but they have either chosen you or you have chosen them yourself.

"They had not been forced on you by a father who had no other way of getting himself and his impoverished Clan solvent."

"But it is all over now," the Duke said. "Margaret is dead and buried."

He said it in a decisive tone which made the Earl look at him sharply.

"All right," he said. "I am not going to ask you for details, nor am I going to pry into what obviously is your own private business. Did you say you had married someone else?"

Before the Duke could answer the door of the Chieftain's Room opened again and Tara came in.

She had been picking flowers from the garden for the Duke's bedroom and she carried a basket full of roses.

Her hair, which had grown longer in the last three weeks, was brilliantly red against the dark oak of the door as she stood for a moment quite still, staring at the Duke sitting in the arm-chair by the window.

Then she gave a little cry of joy which seemed to echo round the room.

"You are up!" she exclaimed. "You are up and dressed! Oh! How do you feel? I do hope it has not made you tired?"

She ran towards him as she spoke, her eyes on his face, and only as she reached him did she realise there was a stranger sitting beside him.

"I am feeling very well as it happens," the Duke answered, "and now Tara, I want to introduce a cousin of mine, the Earl of Strathairdrie. Charles, this is my wife, Tara."

The Earl had been sitting back in his chair and now he sat up straight and stared at Tara with a strange expression on his face.

He did not speak, but sat looking at her, almost as if he was turned to stone.

"How do you do, My Lord."

Tara dropped him a curtsy.

He did not answer and only went on staring until, as she looked at him nervously, the Duke said:

"Charles, as I have just said, this is my wife."

"Who are you?" the Earl asked in a hoarse voice. "What is your name?"

There was something in the way he spoke which made Tara open her eyes in astonishment before she answered:

"My name is Tara ... I have no ... other name."

"My wife is an orphan," the Duke said in an aggressive manner. "She came to me from The Orphanage of the Nameless, which was founded by my Grandmother and your Great-Aunt, the Duchess Harriet."

The Earl ignored the Duke and said to Tara:

"You have no other name?"

She thought the visitor must be rather stupid. He did not seem to grasp what was being said to him.

Because the manner in which he was looking at her made her feel unsure of herself, she said to the Duke:

"I did not know Your Grace had anyone with you. I will go and put these flowers in your bedroom."

"Yes, do that," the Duke said.

Tara would have walked away but the Earl of Strathairdrie put out his hand to stop her.

"No! Wait a moment," he said. "I have something to show you. You have to see it."

He put up his hand and undid his waistcoat and then the buttons of his shirt. Lying on the bare skin of his chest there was a thin chain.

He pulled it forward so that Tara could look at it and she saw it held a miniature.

"Do you see this?" the Earl asked. "Look at it and tell me of whom it reminds you."

Because he told her to do so Tara looked at the miniature.

The painting was somewhat faded, yet it was easy to see it

depicted a very pretty face with blue eyes fringed with dark eye-lashes and framed with red hair.

"Who do you think it is like?" the Earl asked insistently.

"I do not know," Tara said wonderingly.

Then suddenly it struck her that the face was not unlike her own.

She stared at the miniature not liking to put into words what she thought.

"How old are you?" the Earl asked.

"I . . . am . . . eighteen this month."

"And what year were you born?"

"1804."

"I knew it!" the Earl exclaimed.

"What on earth is all this about?" the Duke asked in an irritated tone, "and why should my wife's birth-date be of any interest to you, Charles?"

The Earl gave a deep sigh, pulled the chain round until he could unfasten the clasp and then he drew it from his shirt and held it out to the Duke.

"Look at that," he said.

The Duke took the miniature from him.

"Well?"

"Surely you can see the likeness?" the Earl asked.

"A likeness to Tara?" the Duke enquired. "What are you trying to say?"

"The answer to that question is very simple," the Earl said.

"That is a picture of my wife. . ."

"Your wife!"

There was no doubt the Duke was astonished.

"But Charles, you never had a wife! You have never been married!"

"That is what you and the rest of the family thought," the Earl answered, "but not only had I a wife, Heron, I think at long last I have found my daughter!"

Chapter Six

Tara and the Duke could only stare at the Earl as if he had taken leave of his senses.

Then the Duke asked:

"What are you talking about, Charles? I cannot understand."

The Earl ignored him. His eyes were on Tara's face as he said:

"Why were you called Tara?"

"My Mother had a locket round her neck with the name engraved on it."

"You have it!"

Tara put her hand up to her neck and the Earl said impatiently:

"Let me see."

She pulled the chain up from behind her white collar and slipped it over her head to put the locket into his outstretched hand.

He stared down at it and Tara thought by the expression on his face he was deeply moved.

"If you open it," he said, "you will find there is a lock of my hair inside."

"I wondered ... whose it ... was," Tara said in a voice hardly above a whisper.

The Earl raised his eyes.

"I gave it to your Mother," he said, "because I did not dare give her a wedding-ring."

"She was ... married to ... you?"

It was as if Tara could not say the words and yet they were spoken.

She could barely understand what the Earl meant but knew that something wonderful was happening which made her feel as if she were suddenly being lifted off the ground and into a sunlit sky.

It was so incredible that she could only look at the man sitting in front of her with her locket in his hand and feel she must be in a dream.

"Suppose, Charles, you tell us what all this is about," the Duke said. "I must be very stupid, but I am in fact utterly bewildered."

"I am not surprised!" the Earl replied. "It hardly seems to me possible that I should have searched for my daughter for years and now find her here, married to you."

"Am ... I ... really your ... daughter?" Tara asked.

He put out his hand.

"Come and sit down," he said in a voice he had difficulty in controlling, "and I will tell you the whole story."

There was a chair next to his. Tara sat on it, and the Earl held her hand tightly as if to reassure him she was real and he had in fact found what he had been seeking for so long.

"I was just two months off becoming twenty-one in 1803," he began at length, "when I fell in love."

There was a deep note in his voice which Tara felt was very moving.

"It happened," the Earl continued, "at a Ball I attended at Carlton House, where the Prince of Wales introduced me to the only woman I have ever loved."

"Her name was ... Tara?"

Tara could not help the words coming from her lips. She could hardly bear to wait for the story to unfold.

"Her name was Tara Kildonnon," the Earl replied.

The Duke gave an exclamation.

"Now I know who you are talking about," he said, "I saw her once when I was a young boy. She was very beautiful."

The Earl's fingers tightened on Tara's.

"She looked exactly as you look today," he said to her. "When you came into the room I felt I had stepped back into the past."

"But she was a Kildonnon," the Duke said.

"I know," the Earl answered, "and now you can understand how we suffered. Our love was overwhelming, undeniable and nothing and nobody could prevent us belonging to each other. But we dared not approach either Tara's Father or mine."

"The Clans were bitterly opposed to each other in those days," the Duke said.

"As they have been more or less ever since," the Earl replied. "It was only you, Heron, who were brave enough to say openly you intended to marry a Kildonnon. I think my Father would have killed me if I had even suggested such a thing."

"What did you do?" the Duke asked curiously.

"Tara and I met in secret and I suppose we might have continued to do so had war not broken out again with Napoleon."

"Of course, the armistice came to an end," the Duke murmured.

"Immediately on the declaration of renewed hostilities my Regiment sailed to India.

"We were to join the troops of the Governor, General Lord Wellesley, who was striking at the French-trained armies of the restless Mahrata chiefs."

"You went to India!" Tara exclaimed.

"We arrived just in time for the battle of Laswári, one of the hardest-fought and bloodiest battles in Indian history."

The Earl paused to add:

"My thoughts were, needless to say, concentrated on who was waiting for me in England."

The way in which the Earl spoke told Tara how agonising it had been to leave the woman he loved.

"Because I was frightened that I should lose Tara while I was away," he continued, "I begged her to marry me before I sailed. We decided that when I returned, whatever the consequences, we would tell both our families that we were already man and wife. They could then do nothing about it!"

"So you were married secretly "

"We were married very early one morning and I took my

wife to an hotel where we spent the day together."

The Earl was silent for a moment as if he was looking back into the past.

"I think then I learnt what happiness was really like, and I know Tara felt the same."

He lapsed into silence and the Duke prompted him:

"But you were sent abroad."

"I sailed with my Regiment two days later. I had a few more hours of perfect bliss with Tara, and then swearing undying fidelity, I had to leave her."

He gave a deep sigh before he went on:

"I remember feeling wildly jealous as I had my last glimpse of England, praying that she would not forget me and it would not be long before we could be together."

"What happened?" the Duke asked.

"I could not return to England for three years," the Earl answered, "and then it was only because I had been wounded in battle and was forced to leave the Army. When I got home I found Tara had disappeared."

"Disappeared!" the Duke ejaculated.

"It took me a long time to discover what had happened, as obviously it was impossible for me to question her parents."

His fingers tightened on Tara's as he said:

"At last I found an old maid-servant who had loved her and looked after her ever since she was a child. She told me that three months after I had left, Tara discovered she was going to have a baby."

"But she did not tell her parents?" the Duke questioned.

"How could she?" the Earl asked almost fiercely. "I was a McCraig and, just as I was frightened of my Father, Tara was terrified of hers. He was in fact an obstinate, pig-headed autocrat! Just like a number of other Kildonnons!"

His voice was harsh and then he smiled at Tara.

"They were not all unfortunately, like your mother, lovely, sweet and gentle."

"I wish I could have known her," Tara whispered.

"She would have loved you very deeply," the Earl answered.

"What happened, since she could not tell her parents," the Duke asked, as if he wished to keep the Earl to the point.

"Tara ran away from home with her old maid, Mairi. They found a place where they could live without being discovered, and apparently Tara wrote me a number of letters which I never received telling me what had happened."

The pain in his voice was unmistakable and it was with an obvious effort that he continued:

"One day, Mairi told me, Tara went out shopping. It was a month before the baby was due to arrive and Mairi begged her to be careful. But the woman never saw her again."

"She was involved in an accident," Tara interposed. "Mrs. Barrowfield told me that she was knocked down by a carriage which did not stop and a wheel passed over her. She was carried into the Orphanage and I was born there."

"So that is what happened!" the Earl exclaimed. "I went to every hospital in London to see if there was any record of your birth."

"My mother never regained consciousness," Tara said, "and the Orphanage and the Doctor had no idea who she was."

"She had this locket round her neck?" the Earl asked.

He was still holding the locket in his free hand.

"But she had no ... wedding-ring."

"That was why I gave her the locket, because I dared not give her a ring," the Earl explained. "She was so afraid that her Mother or her Father might find it however carefully it was hidden away."

"So I am not ... a ... bastard?"

Tara could hardly breathe the word, but the Earl heard it and he said almost fiercely:

"You are my daughter, born in wedlock to a wife I loved more than Heaven itself."

"Oh! I am glad! So very, very glad!" Tara cried.

"You must tell me all about yourself," the Earl said. "I have wasted eighteen years in getting to know you and there is so much I want to hear."

"I was just brought up in the Orphanage," Tara

answered. "I would have been sent away as an apprentice when I was twelve, had I not been useful in looking after the little ones. So I stayed on to do that."

"You have never been anywhere else?"

"The first time I left it was when Mr. Falkirk brought me here on His Grace's instructions."

"That is something I do not understand," the Earl said.

The Duke was silent. Then as the Earl waited, obviously intending to have an answer, he said slowly.

"Margaret had been The Kildonnon's choice as to whom I should marry, so after her death I was determined myself to choose my next wife!"

"Then the stories I heard are true!" the Earl said. "It was an act of revenge! That is why you brought Tara here and why she is wearing that hideous charity garment!"

The accusation in his voice was unmistakable and there was also a note of anger in it which made Tara say quickly:

"Please, you must not be angry! It was a good thing I came here because I was able to nurse His Grace when he was wounded."

"I understand you had an accident with your gun," the Earl said almost contemptuously.

The Duke's lips tightened and Tara said:

"That is the ... story I told of what ... occurred because I did not wish to ... encourage the McCraigs to demand vengeance as they certainly would have done if they learnt who had injured their Chief."

The Earl looked at her and smiled.

"Now I am beginning to understand," he said. "It is the sort of thing your Mother would have done. She hated knowing our Clans were always at war with each other. She thought it was cruel and wrong that men should fight! And after she loved me she found a McCraig could be very different from what she had always been told they were like."

"If I am your ... daughter," Tara said softly, "I ... now have a ... name."

"You have indeed!" the Earl answered. "You are the Lady Tara McCraig!"

Tara looked at him wide-eyed.

"Is ... that really ... true?"

"You are as much a McCraig as I am or your husband."

"Yet my ... Mother was a Kildonnon."

"You take your Father's status, but at the same time you may find it difficult to hate and fight against those whose blood runs in your veins, even as mine does."

"I can hardly believe it!" Tara said with shining eyes. "I ... belong, I have a ... family."

"You certainly have!" the Earl answered. "And now, as your Father, I would like to kiss my daughter. It is something, I might tell you, I have often dreamt of doing."

He put his arms round her as he spoke, drew her against him and kissed her on both cheeks.

"You are very thin," he said, "did they not feed you in the Orphanage?"

"Not very well," Tara admitted.

The Earl looked over her head almost furiously at the Duke.

"I thought the place belonged to the family, Heron?"

"According to Falkirk and Tara, it has been very neglected since my Mother died," the Duke replied. "I have already given orders for a number of improvements."

"So I should hope!" the Earl said, "and one obvious thing that has been neglected, Heron, is my daughter's personal appearance."

He paused and then said:

"I think you will agree under the circumstances that I should take her to Edinburgh with me tomorrow. I will fit her out in the clothes that she should be wearing as your wife, and I will also present her to the King."

Tara looked at him wide-eyed.

"Pre ... sent me ... to ... the ... King?"

It was difficult for her to say the words.

"It is only correct that you should be presented on becoming the Duchess of Arkcraig!" the Earl replied. "And as the King is a personal friend of mine I know he will be extremely interested to meet you."

"It will be thrilling," Tara said, "but I hope I shall not do anything wrong to make you ... ashamed of me, or commit ... embarrassing mistakes."

"I will look after you," the Earl said, "and so will my Mother who is in Edinburgh."

Tara's face was alight with excitement. Then she turned nervously to the Duke.

"Can ... I ... go?" she asked. "Please, Your Grace, can ... I ... go?"

He looked at her and she saw that his eyes were as dark and scowling as they had been when she first met him.

"Why not?" he asked coldly. "There is nothing to keep you here."

* * *

Tara stood looking at herself in the mirror and thought it was impossible to believe that she was the same miserable, under-fed orphan who had struggled to keep order in the Orphanage and had at times collapsed from lack of food.

Wearing the beautiful gown her Grandmother had bought for her of white tulle over a rich white satin, it was hard to remember the thread-bare grey cotton dress which had been thrown away as soon as she reached Edinburgh.

Her hair had been arranged by a skilful hairdresser and the maids were waiting to put a bandeau of diamonds on to it.

To this were attached the three Prince of Wales white feathers which she was to wear in the Drawing Room at the Palace of Holyrood House where she was to be presented to the King.

The King had arrived on the 15th August at Leith in the *Royal George* and Tara had felt herself infected by the excitement which had swept over Edinburgh like a tidal-wave.

Forgotten for the moment were the Scottish dislike and distrust of the English; forgotten were the cruel punishments inflicted by the hated Duke of Cumberland after the Battle of Culloden.

Now everyone, from the highest to the lowest, was ready to welcome the first English King who had paid a Royal visit to Scotland since Charles II.

Tara had seen very little of the City since her arrival because she had been kept exceedingly busy by the dressmakers.

They came to her Grandmother's house in unceasing numbers so that she felt one of the most tiring things she had ever had to do was to stand still while garment after garment was fitted, for hours on end.

The results certainly justified anything she might have suffered in the process.

Every day she found new confidence in herself because her appearance was so different and a happiness she had never known before because everyone was so kind to her.

She thought she had loved her Father from the first moment she had met him.

When they drove to Edinburgh, hand in hand, and he told her about his childhood and talked incessantly of her Mother, a feeling of belonging made her thank God over and over again in her heart.

It was wonderful too to find she had a Grandmother and innumerable cousins who welcomed her with a kindness which swept away her shyness.

Only at night did she worry about the Duke and wonder if his wounds had completely healed or if his head was still aching.

It still hurt her when she thought of him to remember how he had sent her away without one word of regret or even of thanks for the way she had nursed him.

She had not expected his gratitude, but she had thought on the last evening at the Castle that he was behaving almost as if he hated her again as he had when she first arrived.

Sometimes she would wake in the night and imagine she was still lying against him with her arms around him and magicking away the pain in his head as she had done when he was first wounded.

He had then not been frightening or overbearing, but only a little boy who was suffering and whom she believed she could help.

Looking at herself in the mirror she wondered whether

if he was here now he would think she was attractive!

Then she told herself despondently that perhaps she would always seem to him nothing but the charity child he had used as an instrument of his revenge.

"Surely the Duke is coming to Edinburgh for the festivities?" Tara would be asked not once but a dozen times a day.

"I do not think he will be well enough," she replied.

"He has been ill?"

"He had an accident, but I am hoping of course he will be well enough to join me."

She was growing quite adept, she realised, in evading difficult questions and talking in the manner which she knew would receive the approval of her Father.

"Your Mother must have been very lovely," her cousins said to her. "We always wondered why Charles never married, for there have been so many beautiful women who would have welcomed him with open arms. But his heart has remained true all these years to his first love."

'It must be wonderful to be loved like that,' Tara thought.

And while she had basked in the attention of her new relatives, while she felt a warmth within herself for them, she could not help feeling she would like something more in her life – the love that her Mother had had for her Father and he for her.

"She was so brave," she told herself, "to defy the feud between the Clans, which was even more intense in those days. If only she had lived she might have joined them together in peace."

She gave a little cry at the pathos of it.

Because just by chance a carriage had knocked her Mother down, a whole chain of events had been put into motion which had ended incredibly with her marrying the Duke.

'I am very lucky,' she thought. 'I might have been apprenticed to someone who was cruel to me, or I might have stayed at the Orphanage for the rest of my life until I died of over-work or starvation.'

But instead she was in Edinburgh, dressed like a Princess

in a fairy story and in an hour's time was to be presented by her Grandmother to His Majesty King George IV.

The Dowager Countess was very impressive in a dress of gold lamé. Her train was trimmed with a gold fringe and she wore a magnificent tiara of pearls and diamonds.

But Tara thought that neither herself nor her Grandmother looked as impressive as the Earl in the full dress of the McCraigs. She knew only one man who could look more splendid and that was the Duke.

As they drove to the Palace of Holyrood House she could not help wishing that the Duke was with them. The presentations were to begin at two o'clock in the Drawing Room and were to continue until half past three.

The Earl had told her that no less than three hundred ladies were to have the privilege of meeting His Majesty and they had all to be in their places before he arrived.

The King had been staying at Dalkeith Palace with the young Duke who was only sixteen.

He was escorted to Edinburgh by troops of the Scots Greys and arrived in Field Marshal's uniform.

The Royal Archers were on duty within the quadrangle of the Palace.

The Drawing Room where the presentations took place was very impressive and the ladies in their diamonds and feathers were resplendent as were the Yeomen of the Guard drawn up round the gallery.

When the time came for Tara to be presented she felt very nervous, but the Countess had smiled at her reassuringly and said :

"There is no-one who looks more beautiful and I would have been proud to present your Mother, as I am to present you."

Tara had practised her curtsy, but she had no idea how many people noticed the grace with which she moved and the beauty of her red hair encircled with a bandeau of diamonds.

But she would have been very unintelligent if she had not realised that her appearance as the new Duchess of Arkcraig caused a sensation amongst the whole assembled company.

Her Father told her afterwards that he was overwhelmed with compliments about her.

Only when the presentation was over and they drove home did Tara wish once again that the Duke had been present.

Before the maids helped her take off her elegant gown she looked at herself in the mirror, at her train of white satin trimmed with tulle and the elegance of the feathers on her head.

Her hair had grown quite a lot in the last month, and was so skilfully arranged that no-one realised how short it really was.

Instead of the reflection of herself, Tara saw for a moment her face framed by the ugly grey cap, her body clothed in the shapeless grey cotton dress with its white collar and heavy black cape that proclaimed loudly she was an object of charity.

"I must forget it, it is all over now!" she told herself. "There is no point in looking back into the past!"

Yet incessantly in her mind was the question: would the Duke ever forget? Would she ever be anything to him other than what she was when he had first brought her to Scotland?

The days after the Drawing Room were filled with the celebrations which had been arranged for His Majesty's visit.

There was a procession to the Castle and immense crowds flocked in from the surrounding country to watch the Royal Pageant and listen to the martial music.

All day and every day Tara could hear the Pipes playing and they still thrilled her as they had the first time she had heard them.

Now she knew she had been right in thinking when she first came to Scotland that she was a Scot and their music was part of her.

The Earl took her to the grand Cavalry Review which took place on the Portobello Sands on the 23rd August.

There, besides the Scottish Cavalry, nearly three thousand

of them, Tara saw the Royal Archers, Members of the Celtic Society and representatives of the Clans.

As she watched them march past the King, she longed for the Duke to be leading the McCraigs as the Duke of Argyll on foot led the Campbells.

As if he knew what she was thinking, the Earl said:

"Heron should be here. I should have insisted on his coming."

"I suppose he was really not well enough," Tara answered.

"Before that damned marriage he would have come however ill he was!" the Earl said irritably.

Then as if he felt he had been tactless, he asked:

"You did not mind my speaking of it?"

"No, of course not," Tara replied, "and I think his hatred of the Kildonnons, which must have been increased by what happened, is harming him both mentally and spiritually."

"You are quite right," the Earl said. "All my life the McCraigs' hatred of the Kildonnons has bedevilled my existence, and I cannot bear that you must suffer as I have from the prejudice and stupidity engendered by that old feud!"

Tara gave a little sigh.

"That is what I feel, Papa! Will you talk to the Duke and try to make him understand that the past should be forgotten and we must think of the future?"

"I will do that," the Earl promised.

"I knew when I first came to Scotland that I wanted to help the poor and those who live in ignorance," Tara said, "and perhaps now I am your daughter, it will be easier. As Mama was a Kildonnon, maybe they will find it easier to accept me."

"I think the Kildonnons will be astonished and delighted," the Earl said with a smile, "when they learn that the new Duchess of Arkcraig is closely connected to them. At the same time perhaps it is a good thing that your McCraig Grandfather is dead!"

"I am glad I shall not have to face him."

"And so am I," the Earl admitted.

They both laughed, but Tara remembered their conversation and thought about it when she went to bed.

The grand highlight of the entertainment arranged for the King was the Ball which would take place at the end of his visit.

The Peers of Scotland were determined to entertain him in the most magnificent manner possible, and because none of them had a ballroom large enough, they had taken over the Assembly Rooms in George Street.

This fine building had two Ballrooms besides a number of other rooms which were used for card assemblies and tea-parties as well as dancing.

Ever since Tara had arrived in Edinburgh, the Peeresses to whom she had been introduced by her Father and Grandmother had talked of little else except the Ball with which they were concerned.

"It is to be the most splendid spectacle that has ever been seen in Scotland," the Countess of Elgin said enthusiastically.

"If that does not impress His Majesty," the Marchioness of Queensbury answered, "then nothing will."

"I can assure you," the Earl said, "that His Majesty is very much looking forward to it."

When he was alone with Tara he said:

"I am looking forward to it too, my dearest, for this is the night you will be able to talk with the King, and I shall be able to introduce you to all my friends. I am very proud of my daughter."

"You have been so kind to me, Papa."

He put his arms around her and kissed her.

"I am so overwhelmingly happy to have found you, and also to know that you are glad to have found me."

"I cannot begin to tell you what it means," Tara said with a little catch in her voice. "I used to tell stories to myself about my Father, but it is far more wonderful to find he is a real person and so distinguished and important."

The Earl laughed and kissed her again.

"You forget that you are now very important in your own right as the Duchess of Arkcraig."

He saw the shadow which passed over Tara's expression and added quietly:

"I am praying things will come right for you, my dearest. I have been fond of Heron ever since he was a small boy and he has great qualities in him. He is a leader of men and a Chieftain of whom the McCraigs can be justly proud."

He paused a moment.

"But I think I am right in saying he has never yet found his heart."

"Mr. Falkirk said he thought he had never really been in love," Tara said.

"I am sure that is true," the Earl answered, "but I cannot believe that anyone could be with you long, my dearest daughter, and not fall in love."

Tara might have doubted such an assertion if she had not found large numbers of young men clustering round her wherever they went, all eager to pay her compliments.

She began to recognise a glint of admiration in their eyes and knew it gave her confidence such as she had always lacked before.

Yet when she returned home, her cheeks flushed, her eyes shining, she would look in the glass and remember the darkness in the Duke's expression.

Then she would be afraid of the future!

The night of the Ball, Tara went up to dress early and after she had bathed in the soft peaty water, scented with flowers, the maids dressed her in the magnificent gown the Earl had specially chosen for the occasion.

It was white, because he said it showed off her red hair to perfection, but it was white with touches of silver.

When she moved she felt as if she was dressed in moonlight and once again she wished the Duke could see her.

The hairdresser had arranged her hair in a new style which was very becoming.

"You must grow it longer, Your Grace," he said. "I cannot think how you allowed it to be cut so short."

He spoke in almost a scolding tone to add:

"None the less it is very pretty and I am prepared to

wager there will be no-one to rival Your Grace in the whole Ballroom."

"Thank you," Tara smiled.

The hairdresser left and Tara looked down at the jewels that lay on the dressing-table.

She had been lent them by her Grandmother, but as the Countess was wearing her own tiara, there was only the bandeau of diamonds for her hair which she had already worn at the Drawing Room.

She picked it up to ask the maids to help her put it on, when there was a knock on the door. Before Tara could answer it opened and she heard someone come into the room.

She knew it was a man and thinking it must be her Father she said:

"I am nearly ready, Papa."

Then as the new-comer moved she saw his reflection in the mirror and was suddenly still.

For a moment she thought she must be imagining his magnificence which might have stepped out of her dreams. Then she turned her head and saw it was really the Duke.

She started to her feet.

"Your ... Grace!"

He did not reply and she moved towards him, her words tumbling over each other as she said:

"I did not ... expect you ... but it is ... wonderful you are ... here ... You are all right? Your wound does not ... hurt you? I hope the ... journey has not been too ... tiring!"

"I am well, Tara," the Duke replied, "and I have brought you the jewels you must wear tonight."

She saw then that he carried in his hand some leather boxes and almost automatically, hardly aware of what she was doing, she took them from him.

"Jewels?" she asked almost stupidly.

"The Arkcraig emeralds," the Duke replied, "which have been in the family for centuries. I think you will find they will enhance your appearance."

"I am sure they ... will," Tara said. "And you are ... coming to the ... Ball?"

"I have every intention of escorting you there."

The Duke spoke coldly and she had the feeling that something had annoyed him.

The maid withdrew tactfully from the room and when they were alone Tara said:

"I am so glad you have ... changed your mind and come to Edinburgh ... I have been ... wishing so often you were ... here."

He looked at her with an expression which she thought was one of disbelief.

"I consider it my duty to meet the King."

"Papa will be very pleased. He has said so often that you would like each other."

The Duke did not speak and after a moment Tara said:

"You are quite ... certain this will not be too ... much for ... you?"

"Quite certain, but anyway my duty is more important than my feelings," the Duke replied. "As I understand, all this junketing will be over after tonight, and I will take you back with me tomorrow."

He turned as he spoke and went from the room as unexpectedly as he had entered it. Tara stood looking after him.

She was not certain what she felt at his sudden appearance. She only knew that she had wanted him and he had come!

Because she was afraid of being late she rang the bell for her maid and hastily began opening the jewel-boxes.

The McCraig emeralds were certainly superb and she was quite certain that when she wore them her jewels would outshine every other Peeress in the room.

At the same time she could not help thinking how valuable they were and how even one stone in the necklace would have fed the orphans properly for months if not years.

She remembered the Duke had said that when they went to London she could give the children toys.

"Now that I am beginning to realise I am really the Duchess of Arkcraig," she said aloud, "there are many other things I will ask for as well."

She had already begun to make a list of beds, floor coverings, kitchen utensils and a hundred other things that were lacking at the Orphanage.

Then with a start she realised that half of the jewels the Duke had brought her were still lying in the boxes and at any minute her husband, her Grandmother and her Father would be waiting for her to drive to the Assembly Rooms.

Afterwards Tara could remember little about the Ball, except that the room was decorated in white and gold and there was a throne hung with red crimson drapery.

Beside it were a number of sofas which were filled with the nobility of Scotland all vying with each other for the Royal visitor's attention.

Although Tara was again presented to His Majesty and he talked to her with great geniality and complimented her Father on having such a beautiful daughter, her mind was continually concerned with the Duke.

The Earl had insisted on her dancing the reels which she had been taught in the evenings before the King's arrival.

As she moved around the Ballroom she kept wondering whether the Duke was watching her and whether he was aware that there were quite a number of gentlemen contending for the privilege of being her partner.

As they all drove back in a carriage to the Countess's house, the Earl said affectionately :

"You were very much admired, my darling, this evening, and His Majesty himself said you were quite the most beautiful person in the Ballroom."

"Thank ... you," Tara said, putting out her hands towards him.

"You must be proud of your wife, Heron," the Countess remarked. "She has been acclaimed as a great beauty ever since she came to Edinburgh."

"So I understand," the Duke said coldly.

*   *   *

They set off early next morning for the journey back to the Castle.

Tara was rather surprised that the Earl made no effort to keep her longer in Edinburgh, but merely said:

"Heron is your husband, my dearest, and if he wants you to return to him then you must obey him."

"When shall I see you again?" Tara asked wistfully.

"Very much sooner than you expect!" the Earl replied. "I have to go back by sea with His Majesty, but as soon as I possibly can, I shall come North and I intend to stay at the Castle whether your husband asks me or not!"

"Of course he will ask you!"

"He may prefer to have you on your own."

Tara did not answer.

She had the unhappy feeling that the Duke not only had no wish to have her on his own, but would be quite content not to have her there at all.

At the same time he had insisted on her returning with him and she wondered if he thought there had been too much gossip about her being in Edinburgh without him.

Whatever the reason, she thought, he was unlikely to confide in her and she would have to go on guessing.

She had so much luggage to take back with her that she was not surprised to find that there were two carriages waiting outside the Countess's house.

What she had not expected was that there would also be a riding-horse for the Duke. Tara looked at it in consternation.

"You must not ride!" she exclaimed, "it will be far too much for you! You know what the Doctor said, you were to do as little as possible for several months."

"I have every intention of riding!" the Duke replied. "If there is one thing I really dislike, it is being cooped up in a carriage for hours on end!"

"You will get so tired," Tara expostulated.

He had made no answer, only turned away from her to say good-bye to the Countess and to the Earl.

"Your visit has been so brief, Heron," the latter said, "that I have hardly had time to congratulate you on your marriage, or to decide what I will give my son-in-law as a wedding-present."

"You have certainly been very generous to my wife," the Duke said with a glance at the innumerable trunks that were being piled on to the second carriage.

"They were presents to my daughter," the Earl corrected. "I still have to think of something you both need. It will occupy my thoughts all the time I am trying hard not to be sea-sick in the *Royal George*!"

They both laughed. Then the Earl put his arms round Tara and held her close against him.

"If you only knew, my dearest little daughter, what it has meant to me to find you!" he said. "There are so many things that I want for you, but most of all, I want you to be happy."

"I shall try to be that," Tara answered.

She knew her Father understood the difficulties that existed between her and the Duke, and she felt very forlorn sitting alone in the carriage waving until the Earl and her Grandmother were out of sight.

The Duke was riding ahead so she could watch him through the window and notice how magnificent he looked upon a horse.

'He is so handsome,' she thought. 'Papa is right: he is exactly what a Chieftain should be.'

And then almost mockingly a voice seemed to say:

"A Chieftain without a heart."

"He will be afraid to love after what happened to him in his first marriage," Tara told herself.

And yet she could well believe he was able to make any woman's heart beat faster just because he was so handsome and so outstanding.

"If only I knew more about men and life," Tara murmured and knew how ignorant she was.

She had felt shy and a little embarrassed when the gentlemen in Edinburgh had paid her fulsome compliments and thought she would gladly exchange them all for one word of kindness from the Duke.

"He is my husband, and I want him to like me, and I want

him to admire me! I want him to think I am attractive!"

She went on watching him through the open window and knew that neither in the crowded Ballroom nor anywhere else in Edinburgh had she seen a man that she had admired more.

Who else could make her feel as the Duke had done when he came into her room last night bringing her the jewels he wanted her to wear?

She had known then that her heart seemed to turn over in her breast and something very exciting came to life within her. It was almost as if the room seemed ablaze with light because he was there.

She had felt it difficult to breathe from the moment she saw him reflected in the mirror.

"Because it was such a surprise!" she told herself.

All evening she knew she had been vividly conscious of him. Because he was in the Ballroom she found it hard to attend to what her partners were saying to her, or to remember the steps of the reels.

Even when she was talking to the King, part of her mind had been occupied with the Duke who was standing near them.

She was wondering whether he would approve of what she was saying or would disapprove, and whether he admired her as the King did.

Everything that had happened while she was in Edinburgh was thrilling, she thought, but last night had been different.

It was different because the Duke had been with her, and her feelings were more intense because he was there.

He had slept in the room next to hers and she had longed when they went up to bed to go in and ask him if she could look at the wound on his arm, and perhaps rebandage it for him.

But he had not suggested she should do so when they were climbing the stairs, and then she had heard his door close decisively a second after she had closed hers.

It seemed to her then as if they were separated by something far more than a wall of bricks and mortar.

"I am married to him," Tara said aloud.

But she knew it was not only her anxiety over his wounded arm which made her want to go to his bedroom as she had done when he was ill.

It was because she wanted to be alone with him, to talk with him.

She sat back in the carriage as the horses carried them swiftly over the firm good roads leading out of Edinburgh.

They had one night to stay on the way. When eventually they arrived at a Posting Inn, Tara was tired after being so late at the Ball.

It was not as well appointed as those she had stayed in in England with Mr. Falkirk on the way North, but it was quite comfortable.

The Duke must have engaged the best rooms on his way to Edinburgh, for the Landlord was expecting them, and a private sitting-room was at their disposal.

Tara washed, changed and went downstairs to find the Duke waiting for her.

"You must be very tired," she said with concern in her voice. "I am sure it was far too long for you to be in the saddle."

"I am tired, but not unduly so," he admitted, "and we shall be home by tomorrow evening."

"Perhaps you will drive with me tomorrow?" Tara asked timidly.

As she spoke she knew how much she wanted him to do so, not only from the point of his health, but because she could be with him.

"I will see how I feel," the Duke answered evasively.

The Landlord hurried in with the large well-cooked dinner and it was possible to speak of only common-place matters while the servants were in the room.

When finally they had finished and the Duke was sitting back with a glass of brandy in his hand, Tara said:

"I am so ... glad that you came to ... Edinburgh."

"Why?" the Duke enquired.

She felt disconcerted at his question.

"So many people ... asked after you, and it was only ...

right that you should represent the ... McCraigs."

"I am sure your Father was a very adequate substitute in my absence," the Duke answered.

"But it was not the same as your being there," Tara said.

Her eyes met his and it seemed to her as if he was asking her a question but she did not know what it was.

He seemed about to say something and then abruptly he changed his mind.

"If anyone is tired," he said, "it must be you, Tara, after dancing all night and every night, which must certainly have been a change from your previous existence. Go to bed and when we reach the Castle we will talk of things that concern us both."

Tara's eyes widened and then as the Duke had risen to his feet she rose too.

She wanted to ask him what he meant; she wanted to stay; but he raised her hand perfunctorily to his lips and there was nothing she could do but curtsy and leave him.

Only as she reached her own bedroom she wondered with a feeling of horror if after all he had no use for her as his wife and wanted to be rid of her.

Almost as though she saw the scene that might take place in front of her eyes, she could imagine him finding excuses for her to live with her father; for her to leave the Castle and spend her time either in London or Edinburgh.

"Is that what he intends to suggest?"

And even as the questions seemed to crowd in on her — questions to which she had no answers — she knew that what she wanted more than anything else was to stay at the Castle!

To stay with the Duke because she loved him!

Chapter Seven

When Tara saw the Castle silhouetted against the sky, she felt a sudden surge of gladness that she was home.

The dark clouds which had covered the sky for most of the day had suddenly broken, and for the last hour there had been scuds of rain carried by a cold wind which made her feel increasingly anxious about the Duke.

She had hoped, despite the fact that he had again insisted upon riding when they set off that morning, that he would change his mind when it was obvious he would get wet and join her in the carriage.

But he had ridden ahead and she could only watch him anxiously through the closed window and hope he would not catch a chill.

She could not help thinking that perhaps the reason why he preferred the roughness of the weather to her company was that he did not wish to talk intimately with her.

"But I must talk to him ... I must!" she told herself. "There is so much we have to ... plan for the ... future."

Even as she spoke she wondered if in fact there was any future for her at the Castle with the Duke.

During the night, when she had admitted to herself that she loved him, she had felt despairingly that she would never be able to sweep away the expression of darkness from his eyes or make him care for her.

She did not demand his love: that was too much to expect.

All she longed for was to be with him and for him to talk to her gaily and easily, as he had the day before he took her up Ben Ark to look at the view and nearly lost his life.

"I was happy then," she told herself, "happier than I have ever been in my whole life."

Although it seemed ungrateful, she knew now that even the excitement and joy of being in Edinburgh with her Father was not enough to make her really happy.

'I am greedy to want more,' she thought.

But her longing for the Duke could not be talked away by words, and she knew that her whole body ached for him with a helpless despairing yearning that made her feel as if the future was menacing.

Intent on watching him she was relieved when they turned towards the valley and she saw him ride away into the driving rain and she knew that he intended to reach the Castle more quickly than the carriage could do by going across the moors.

But there was no doubt that he must by now be soaked to the skin, and her anxiety for him took away the happiness that rose irresistibly within her at the sight of the great stone battlements and towers surmounted by the Duke's flag flying in the wind.

"I am home!" Tara cried in her heart and felt almost as if a voice asked the question:

"But for how long?"

Mr. Falkirk was waiting for her on the steps as the carriage drew to a standstill.

As a footman opened the door Tara jumped out, holding out both her hands to him.

"Welcome home!" he said, and she saw the delight in his eyes.

"It is wonderful to be back!" she replied and meant it.

"It is good to see you," he answered, "and you are looking very beautiful!"

She had forgotten in her concern for the Duke that her appearance would be a surprise to Mr. Falkirk.

In her fashionable bonnet trimmed with feathers and her elegantly fitting green silk coat over a matching gown she looked very different from the charity child who had left the Castle three weeks before.

Tara's thoughts were however only of the Duke.

"His Grace? He must have been very wet," she said anxiously.

"I insisted that he should take off his wet clothes and have a hot bath," Mr. Falkirk replied.

She gave a little sigh of relief.

"He would ride instead of travelling in the carriage."

"I hope His Grace will have the good sense to rest before dinner and you should do the same."

"But there is so much I want to tell you," Tara protested.

"I shall be able to hear it later," Mr. Falkirk reassured her. "His Grace has very kindly asked me to dine with you."

"That will be delightful!" Tara exclaimed.

But although her voice was enthusiastic she could not help wondering if the Duke had issued the invitation because he did not wish to be alone with her.

Mr. Falkirk escorted her up the stairs and she chatted away to him, telling him how gracious the King had been and of the gaiety of the festivities in Edinburgh.

"The Clans looked magnificent at the Grand Review," she said, "but how I wish the Duke could have led the Mc-Craigs."

"I think he wished it himself," Mr. Falkirk answered, "but after you left he was really not well enough to travel until the actual day he departed."

"He had a relapse?" Tara asked sharply.

"Not exactly," Mr. Falkirk replied. "But he seemed low and depressed. Hector said he was not sleeping well and I suspect he was in pain."

"I should not have left him," Tara said beneath her breath, then heard again the note in the Duke's voice as he said:

"There is nothing to keep you here."

The maids were waiting for her in her Bed-room, and while she undressed she found it difficult to think of anything but the Duke in the next room.

She hoped he was asleep and she longed to look for herself and make certain that he was in fact resting.

But the communicating door between their rooms seemed as firmly shut as if it had been locked, and after she had bathed and the maids had left her she looked at it for a long time before finally she fell asleep.

Two hours later she awoke refreshed and chose one of

her prettiest new gowns in which to dine with the Duke and Mr. Falkirk.

As she walked into the Chieftain's Room to find both men waiting she watched the Duke's face hoping she would see the same glint of admiration in his eyes that she had noticed among her admirers in Edinburgh.

To her disappointment the Duke was not looking at her but was showing Mr. Falkirk a printed memento of the King's visit and pointing out to him the occasions on which the McCraigs had been present.

Because she suddenly felt piqued by his lack of interest Tara deliberately stood in front of him and said :

"Mr. Falkirk has admired my new clothes. I hope Your Grace approves of this gown. It was greatly admired the only other time I have worn it."

"That I can well believe," the Duke replied.

She was not certain from his answer whether he approved or not, and the expression on his face told her nothing.

Disappointed she plunged into a conversation with Mr. Falkirk, conscious all the time that the one person she wished to talk to was her husband.

When dinner was announced they went into the Dining-Room and Tara realised the cooks had made a special effort to produce a superlative meal to celebrate her return.

She tried to do justice to the many dishes, but it was hard to attend to what she was eating while every nerve in her body was tense because she was sitting next to the Duke.

He did not look particularly tired, she thought, although she was sure he must be after riding for two days. But she thought, although she was not certain, that he was glad to be home.

Because she loved him she felt she should be perceptive not only to his moods but also to his thoughts.

A gust of wind shook the windows and Tara said with a smile to Mr. Falkirk :

"I am glad the Duke and I are not on Ben Ark tonight!"

"I expect you would keep His Grace warm and dry as you did before," he replied.

The Duke looked at Tara.

"Did it rain after I was shot?"

"Yes . . . we had quite a downpour."

"Yet you kept me dry? How?"

The colour rose up Tara's cheeks and she could not look at the Duke. He was waiting for her answer and after a moment she said in a low voice:

"I . . . c . covered . . . you with my . . . cloak."

"And held me in your arms?"

"Y . yes."

She was afraid that he thought it an impertinence. Then before he could speak again there was the high, sweet tone of the Pipes!

When dinner was over and they had talked for a short while in the Chieftain's Room, Tara rose to her feet.

"I think we are both tired, after two days travelling," she said to the Duke, "and I am sure you should rest."

She felt he resented her concern for him and quickly, in case he should say something that would hurt her she curtsied to Mr. Falkirk and as he raised her hand to his lips she asked:

"You are pleased to have us back?"

"The Castle seemed very empty when you were away," he replied.

There was a sincerity in his voice which made her smile.

"Thank you," she murmured and felt he had given her a little comfort to take to bed with her.

Mrs. McCraig had lit the fire in her bed-room because the rain was beating against the windows driven by a wind from the North.

"It's been cold these last two days, Your Grace," she said, "and I hear the weather was none too good in Edinburgh either."

"His Majesty got wet on several occasions," Tara answered. "I am hoping His Grace will not catch a cold after riding here in the rain."

"His Grace was never one to worry about the elements," Mrs. McCraig replied complacently.

She opened the door, curtsied and bade Tara good-night. When she had gone the room seemed very quiet.

Tara blew out the candles and got into bed.

She had no wish to-night to read. Her eyes were on the communicating door and she wondered whether the Duke had given her a thought as he retired for the night.

She remembered the times when she had stayed with him re-bandaging his arm and being at his side whenever he was restless. She wondered if he remembered it too.

'He has no need for me now,' she thought despairingly and wondered what they would say to each other tomorrow.

Supposing he told her that she was free to live with her Father if she preferred to do so?

She felt her spirits sink despondently as she knew it would be impossible to tell him the real reason why she wanted to stay at the Castle.

How could she ever tell him of her love? How could he ever understand that having come to him unwillingly she now found that he filled her life, her thoughts and her very soul so that there was no room for anyone else.

"I love him! I love him! Oh, God, I love him! Let him learn to have a little affection for me!" she prayed. "Let him want me to stay, if only so that I may bring the Clans together and there need be no more fighting."

She shut her eyes while she prayed and because of the intensity of her prayer the tears were near to the surface as she opened them again.

Then suddenly she was very still for without her hearing him the Duke had come into her room.

She could see him standing just inside the communicating door, and in the firelight she noticed he was wearing a long dark robe which she remembered.

For a moment it was impossible to breathe, let alone speak. Then the Duke said:

"My head is aching."

Tara sat up in bed.

"I am not surprised. How could you have been so foolish as to ride for two whole days when the Doctor had said you were to be careful of yourself for as many months?"

The Duke did not answer, but he put his hand up to his forehead.

"I will magic it away as I have done before," Tara said. "Would you like to sit in the chair?"

"I am cold, and there is no fire in my room," the Duke replied.

"You must have caught a chill," Tara cried. "Lie down on the bed and cover yourself with the eiderdown. I will make up the fire."

She climbed out of bed as she spoke and walked towards the big fireplace to pick up a log from a basket of them lying to one side of it.

She had forgotten as she did so that she was not wearing one of the thick calico nightgowns which she had worn all her life, but instead was clad in a diaphanous gown of the finest lawn inset with lace which her father had bought for her in Edinburgh.

In the light from the fire the transparency of it revealed every soft curve of her body.

She put several logs on the fire, then turned towards the bed.

As she reached it she found the Duke was lying not on the outside as she had suggested but inside the bed and in the very centre of it.

She looked at him in perplexity, realising that the bed was so wide that from the side it would be difficult for her to reach his forehead.

"I think you will have to move nearer to the side," she suggested.

"I would be more comfortable if you held me as you did when I was wounded on Ben Ark and as you were doing when I regained consciousness," the Duke replied.

The colour burned in Tara's face.

"I ... I did not ... know you were ... aware of what was ... happening," she stammered a little incoherently.

"It was the easiest way for you to massage my forehead," he said, "as it is now. Besides, despite the fire, the room is still cold."

"Very well," Tara agreed, feeling she must do as he wished.

She meant as he was inside the bed to lie on top of it,

but somehow, she was not certain how it happened, as she moved she found herself between the sheets and the Duke pulled the blankets over them both.

She lay against the pillows and he put his head on her breast so that she was holding him in exactly the same way that she had when he was unconscious.

Only now one of his arms was outstretched over her body.

She had been concerned then only because he was ill. But while she told herself she was thinking only of alleviating his headache she could feel a thrill of excitement run through her like quicksilver.

It was because she was so close to him and because his head was heavy against her as it had been before.

"I must be careful not to make him aware that I feel any different from the way I felt then," she warned herself.

She laid her fingers against his forehead running them very gently from his eye-brows to his hair using the mesmeric rhythm which she had found alleviated his pain in the past.

"That is better," he said in a tone of satisfaction, "much better!"

"You must take more care of yourself. Mr. Falkirk did not think you were really well enough to come to Edinburgh."

"You were not here to tell me what not to do," the Duke replied.

"Perhaps it was ... wrong of me to ... leave you," Tara said, "but you seemed so much better and you did not ... want me."

She could not help there being a little throb in her voice as she said the last two words.

The hurt was there, still a deep wound which she knew was unforgettable.

He did not answer and after a moment she asked:

"Is your arm hurting you?"

"Not my arm," he replied, "the pain is in my heart."

Tara started.

"In your heart? That might be serious. Have you informed the Doctor?"

"No."

"How long have you had it?"

"A long time. Ever since you left."

"Why did you not tell me when we were in Edinburgh? There are Specialists there in every branch of medicine and you could have seen one of them."

"They would not have been able to help me."

"How can you be sure of that? Is it bad?"

"Very bad – in fact it has been agonising!"

Tara's arms tightened about him and her fingers dropped from his forehead.

"Listen," she said urgently, "this cannot be allowed to continue. Pease let me ring the bell and send a groom to fetch the Doctor."

"I have already told you – he cannot help."

"Then what can we do?" Tara asked helplessly.

"I was wondering if you would cure me."

"I will do anything ... anything to ease the pain."

"Are you sure of that?"

The Duke moved suddenly, supporting himself on his elbow, and Tara found that instead of holding him in her arms she had slipped back against the pillows and he was looking down at her.

It was hard to see the expression in his eyes as the fire was behind him and because she was thinking only of his illness she said:

"You cannot go on suffering. It might be ... dangerous. I must do ... something!"

"That is what I thought you would say," the Duke answered.

"Then ... what can I do?" she asked.

Even as she asked the question she was aware that his head was just above her and she felt, because he seemed to overshadow her, curiously weak and helpless.

She was no longer in command of the situation – he was.

She looked up at him trying to see his eyes, aware that because he was so near to her, her heart was thumping frantically in her breast.

"Must I tell you in words?" the Duke asked.

Then his lips came down on hers and held her captive.

For a moment she was too astonished to move or breathe. Then as he kissed her she felt as if the world stood still and there was nothing but the wonder of his lips.

She could no longer think but only feel as if her whole body was invaded by a glory that was so rapturous, so ecstatic that it was indescribable.

It seemed to sweep through her like the golden rays of the sun, like the rainbow she had seen over the valley.

She was blinded by its glory and she vibrated to the beauty of it.

She was no longer herself but part of the shimmering colours that came in some indescribable manner from the Duke and the whole splendour and magnificence of him.

She had never known in all her starved, lonely life that it was possible to feel as if she was opening like a flower to an incredible warmth and magic.

She knew what she was feeling was love; the love which she had for the Duke; intensified until it was part of the sun, the sky and the glory that she had felt because she was Scottish.

The Duke raised his head.

"Now do you understand?" he asked and his voice was very low and deep.

"I ... I was afraid you meant to ... send me away."

"Send you away?" he echoed. "I fetched you home because I could not bear to stay here another moment without you."

"I . is that ... true?"

"How could you ever think of leaving me when you knew how much I wanted you?"

"How was I to know ... that?" Tara asked. "You never ... told me so. You said there was ... nothing to keep me here."

"I was furious that you should wish to go away even though it was with your Father. You are mine, Tara. I brought you to Scotland, and I married you."

"But you did not ... w . want me," Tara murmured. "I

was only ... the instrument of your ... revenge."

"That was the first reason," the Duke agreed. "But when you looked after me I began to realise every day you meant more to me than anyone had ever meant to me before in my whole life."

Tara gave a little sigh.

"If only I had ... known."

The Duke made a sound that was almost a laugh.

"I was fighting my love every inch of the way, I wanted to go on fighting for my revenge. But you enchanted me, and if you like – bewitched me!"

"I cannot ... believe it!"

There was a sob behind the words. Then Tara said:

"I am so ignorant ... will you teach me ... so that you will not be ... ashamed of me?"

"I should never be ashamed of you, my darling," the Duke replied, "but there is so much I want to teach you."

"How to ... love you as you ... wish to be loved."

"All I want is for you to hold me in your arms against your breasts, to give me the magic of your touch and the softness of your lips."

"That ... is what I have longed to ... do but I thought you might think it ... impertinent."

"But now you know I think it the most perfect thing which has ever happened to me."

Tara drew in her breath from sheer happiness. The Duke's lips moved over her cheek. Then when she longed for him to kiss her lips again she suddenly gave a little cry.

"What is it?" he asked.

"I have just thought ... the curse ... it is finished!"

"What curse?" the Duke asked.

"The curse of the Clan when you married someone who was not a McCraig."

The Duke laughed.

"I cannot believe you have been listening to that nonsense which that wicked old woman keeps screaming at me?"

"Mr. Falkirk said it was nonsense too," Tara said, "but when you were shot on top of Ben Ark and I held you close to save you from getting wet, I was afraid ... desperately afraid that the ... curse might have ... killed you."

"I do not believe in curses," the Duke replied, "but I believe in you, my darling one, and I know that you are everything I have always wanted and which I thought never to find."

"The Duchess Margaret died," Tara persisted, "you were shot by a Kildonnon, and it all came about ... because you did not ... marry a McCraig."

"Now I have married one," the Duke said.

"Just by chance," she answered, "I might really have been the ... Sassenach you thought I was."

"If you can believe in curses, you can also believe in fate," the Duke answered. "It was fate, my precious, that you should come to me from the Orphanage. It was fate that Charles found his long-lost daughter."

His lips moved against the corner of Tara's mouth, as he said fiercely :

"If your Father thinks he is going to take you away from me, then he is very much mistaken!"

"He wants me to be ... happy," Tara whispered.

It was difficult to speak for she was thrilling not only to the Duke's lips but also to the touch of his hand.

She never imagined it was possible to feel so many strange and wonderful sensations sweeping over her as if they were flames moving up her body, so intense that they were half-pain and half an incredible joy.

"And can I make you happy?" the Duke asked.

"All I ... want is to be with you ... to look at you ... to hear you talking to me and to know that you care for me ... just a little."

"I love you!" the Duke said positively, "and that, Tara, is something I have never said before to any woman. I love you! I do not know how it happened, but when you went to Edinburgh you took my heart with you. The pain of losing it has been indescribable!"

"I will ... try to take away the ... pain," Tara whispered.

His mouth came down on hers and she felt that like the music of the Pipes the glory of what they were both feeling surged outwards to fill the Castle and become part of the wild, beautiful country outside.

* * *

The fire was dying down but by the light of its red ashes the Duke could see the glimmer of gold on Tara's curls as he asked:

"Have I made you happy, my little love?"

"So happy that I feel as if my whole ... being is ... singing with the ... wonder of it."

"You are so soft, sweet and adorable, that I am desperately afraid of losing you. Are you sure that you still love me?"

"That is a question I wanted to ask you, because you are so magnificent, so splendid and so important that I cannot believe I really belong to you."

"You are mine and I love everything about you, not only your beauty – and you are the most beautiful person I have ever seen – but also your kindness, your understanding and perhaps most of all, your compassion – even for the Kildonnons."

"Have you forgotten ..?" Tara began, only to realise that the Duke was teasing her.

He pulled her closer to him.

"We must unite the Clans," he said. "You are right – absolutely right in thinking there must be no more fighting, no more feuding, no more vengeance between our people."

He kissed her before he went on:

"To-morrow we will go over and see The Kildonnon and tell him who you are. Although I am quite certain he knows it already."

"Has someone told him?"

The Duke laughed.

"Have you not realised, my adorable one, that in Scotland news is carried on the wind? There is no need for newspapers. Everything is known almost as soon as it happens. I am quite certain The Kildonnon will be aware by now that the Duchess of Arkcraig has his blood in her veins."

"And yours," Tara said quickly. "I am half a McCraig."

"You are my wife and that is all that matters," the Duke

replied. "Mine completely and I will share you with no-one, whatever Clan they belong to."

"That is what I ... want you to ... feel. Is it really ... true? That you love me, and I am here in the Castle, close to you?"

She gave a sound that was almost a sob.

"Supposing I ... wake up to find it has all been a ... wonderful dream and I am in the ... Orphanage and the children are crying because there is not enough ... food for breakfast?"

The Duke held her so close against him that she could hardly breathe.

"You are awake, my precious. You are in my arms and you will never be lonely or hungry again."

He kissed her eyes before he went on :

"We will make the Orphanage a model of its kind. I shall always bless the fact that it was there and was owned by the family, otherwise I might never have found you."

"Supposing I had been ... apprenticed when I was ... twelve?" Tara whispered.

The Duke's lips moved over her skin.

"It has all been a plan thought out by Someone greater than ourselves," he said gently. "I am sure that is what your Father thinks too."

"He is so happy to have found me, he believes it is God who brought us together."

"You told me to forget the past, my lovely one," the Duke said, "and you have to forget it, too. We have so much to do together in the future."

"You know I will do ... anything that you ... ask of me."

"That is going to be a great deal," the Duke answered. "When you left for Edinburgh I realised how lonely I had been living here. Although I had so many people dependent upon me and so many affairs to occupy my time, my mind was alone, darling, and my heart was left out in the cold."

"It will never be again," Tara murmured. "I will love you ... always ... completely and with every ... part of me. There is no-one else but you. You fill my whole life."

"That is what I want you to say," the Duke answered, "but I warn you, my lovely little wife, I will be very jealous."

She looked up at him with a smile he could just see by the light from the fire.

"Jealous?" she questioned.

"You are too beautiful," he answered. "When I saw you in Edinburgh I realised I could not bear you to be there for even one more day. There were too many temptations."

Tara laughed softly.

"There are many fine men, but no-one who looked like ... you. I kept thinking how you would outshine any other man in the Palace, in the Ball-Room or at the Grand Review."

The Duke drew her closer in his arms and now he was kissing her again, kissing her lips, her neck, her shoulders and lastly her rose-tipped breasts.

"I love you!" he said fiercely. "I want to keep on telling you so, but there are no words in which to express what I feel for you or how much I need you."

"As I ... need you," Tara whispered. "But I am so afraid of ... disappointing you."

"You will never do that, because we belong to each other. Not only is your blood my blood and your heart my heart, but there is something else, my precious, something which springs from our souls and which I think you heard in the music of the Pipes."

"That is what I was ... thinking too."

"We think the same and we are the same," the Duke said. "That is why whatever the difficulties, whatever the problems ahead we shall surmount them because having found each other we are both of us complete."

Tara gave a sigh of sheer happiness.

Then because the Duke was kissing her again, passionately and demandingly, it was impossible to think of anything but him.

Their love was like the rainbow, it enveloped them with a divine radiance which also held a message of hope for the Clans.

Other Books by Barbara Cartland

Romantic Novels, over 200, the most recently published being:
Conquered by Love
Never Laugh at Love
The Secret of the Glen
The Dream and the Glory
The Proud Princess
Hungry for Love
The Heart Triumphant
The Disgraceful Duke
The Taming of Lady Lorinda
Vote for Love
The Mysterious Maid-Servant
The Magic of Love
Kiss the Moonlight
Love Locked In
The Marquis who Hated Women
Rhapsody of Love
Look, Listen and Love
A Duel With Destiny
The Wild, Unwilling Wife
Punishment of a Vixen

Autobiographical and Biographical
The Isthmus Years 1919–1939
The Years of Opportunity 1939–1945
I Search for Rainbows 1945–1966
We Danced All Night 1919–1929
Ronald Cartland (with a foreword by Sir Winston Churchill)
Polly, My Wonderful Mother

Historical
Bewitching Women
The Outrageous Queen (The Story of Queen Christina of Sweden)
The Scandalous Life of King Carol
The Private Life of King Charles II
The Private Life of Elizabeth, Empress of Austria
Josephine, Empress of France
Diane de Poitiers
Metternich – the Passionate Diplomat

Sociology
You in the Home
The Fascinating Forties
Marriage for Moderns
Be Vivid, Be Vital
Love, Life and Sex
Vitamins for Vitality
Husbands and Wives
Etiquette
The Many Facets of Love
Sex and the Teenager
The Book of Charm
Living Together
The Youth Secret
The Magic of Honey
Barbara Cartland's Book of Beauty and Health
Men are Wonderful

Cookery
Barbara Cartland's Health Food Cookery Book
Food for Love
Magic of Honey Cookbook

Editor of
The Common Problems by Ronald Cartland (with a preface by the
Rt. Hon. The Earl of Selborne, P.C.)

Drama
Blood Money
French Dressing

Philosophy
Touch the Stars

Radio Operetta
The Rose and the Violet (music by Mark Lubbock),
performed in 1942.

Radio Plays
The Caged Bird: An episode in the Life of Elizabeth, Empress of
Austria. Performed in 1957.

Verse
Lines on Life and Love